The Goodenoughs
Get in Sync

A Story for Kids

About the Tough Day When Filibuster Grabbed Darwin's Rabbit's Foot

and the Whole Family Ended Up in the Doghouse

An Introduction to Sensory Processing Disorder

and Sensory Integration

by Carol Stock Kranowitz, M.A.

author of *The Out-of-Sync Child* **and** *The Out-of-Sync Child Has Fun*

illustrated by T.J. Wylie

❋ Sensory RESOURCES LLC

Las Vegas

CIP data is available from the publisher or the Library of Congress

Cover and interior illustrations by T. J. Wylie

Cover photo: © Beverly Rezneck

First Edition, November, 2004

Published by

Sensory
RESOURCES LLC
2500 Chandler Avenue, Suite 3
Las Vegas, NV 89120-4064
Tel. 888-357-5867
Fax 702-891-8899
Email Info@SensoryResources.com
www.SensoryResources.com

ISBN 978-1-931615-17-9
Printed in Canada

10 9 8 7 6 5 4 3 2 1

To the boys and girls

who feel that being in the world is a struggle

and want to know why

Contents

Preface

Picture this scene: June 2003, Washington, DC, the noisy exhibit hall at a conference for children with special needs. Hundreds of parents, teachers, therapists, and vendors bustle around. Music plays, balloons sway, loud speakers blare, and the bouquet of hotdogs and coffee permeates the air.

Being a sensory seeker, I like the hullabaloo. Of course, I know that many people find the tactile, visual, and auditory commotion unmanageable. As I move from booth to booth, testing fingerpaints and tasting sourballs, I think about how this busy milieu would affect some of the special children I've taught. Little Betsy would be lunging for the play equipment and wallowing in the Theraputty.™ Darwin would go into fight, flight, fright, or freeze mode in response to the sensory overload. Edward would pay no attention at all…

Amid the hubbub, I spot a friend, Nika Hamblin. Nika is the mother of a child with sensory processing problems and a distributor of Discovery Toys. We are delighted to meet again and to catch up with each other's busy lives. As we chat, I squeeze one of her tactile toys with one hand and shake a pleasant-sounding rattle with the other.

"You have great toys," I say.

"You know something really great we could use?" she asks.

"No, what?"

Nika says, "A book. There are plenty of books for kids to read about autism and all kinds of developmental delays and disabilities. But there is nothing for kids to read about sensory processing. My son Spencer has sensory issues, and he can read, and he needs a book to help him understand why he acts the way he does. A kids' book would fill a huge gap. So many children and parents I know really need it."

"Great idea," I say cheerfully.

"So, will you write it?" she asks.

"Uh," I say.

"Please think about it. Soon," she says.

"But, Nika, a parent should write that book. Someone who lives 24/7 with a child who has sensory processing disorder."

"No," she says shaking her head. "You."

And now you have it—a "chapter book" for 8- to 12-year-olds that tells the tale of five family members, each with a different sensory processing challenge, and their naughty dog. The charming illustrations are by T.J. Wylie.

Thank you, Nika and other parents. Thank you, kids. You have given me so many great ideas! This book is for you.

Carol Kranowitz
Autumn 2004, Bethesda, Maryland

Acknowledgments

These are the children, parents, therapists, and other friends who helped fine-tune this story: Jessica Abrams; Paula Aquilla, BSc, OT; Julia Berry, MA; Katherine Gilpin; Nika and Spencer Hamblin; Diana Henry, MS, OTR/L; Jane Koomar, PhD, OTR/L, FAOTA; Diane Lewis, MA, CCC-SLP; Lucy Jane Miller, PhD, OTR, FAOTA; Kathleen Morris, MS, CCC-SLP; Troy Pfefferle; Susan Snell, MS, LMFT; Jill Spokojny, OTR; and Mark Zweig, MD.

These are the therapists whose concepts and expressions add flavor to this book: Genevieve Jereb, OTR, and Colleen Hacker, MS, OTR (Gravity Monster); Deanna Iris Sava, MS, OTR/L, and Elizabeth Haber, MS, OTR/L (Heavy Work Activities); Nancy Kashman, BS, LOTR, and Janet Mora, MA, CCC-SLP (Internal Eyes); Mary Sue Williams, OTR, and Sherry Shellenberger, OTR (Just Right); Alvin Chan, OTR (OK vs. not OK); and Patricia Wilbarger, MEd, OTR, FAOTA, and Julia Leigh Wilbarger, OTR (Sensory Diet).

This is the artist whose expressive illustrations bring all the Goodenoughs to life: T. J. Wylie.

These are the editors and publishers at Sensory Resources whose vision and skill guided the production of this book: David E. Brown, JD, and Polly A. McGlew, JD.

With my whole heart, I thank them all.

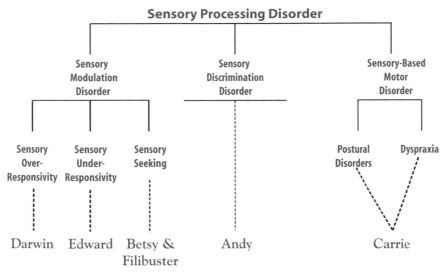

Sensory Processing Disorder

Sensory Modulation Disorder — Sensory Discrimination Disorder — Sensory-Based Motor Disorder

Sensory Over-Responsivity — Sensory Under-Responsivity — Sensory Seeking

Postural Disorders — Dyspraxia

Darwin — Edward — Betsy & Filibuster — Andy — Carrie

This chart shows the types of sensory processing problems that affect each member of the Goodenough family.

The Goodenough Family

Andy   Betsy   Carrie   Darwin   Edward   Filibuster

Visit the Goodenough Family online at
www.TheGoodenoughs.com

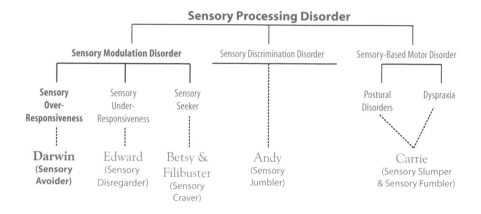

Sensory Processing Disorder

| Sensory Modulation Disorder | | | Sensory Discrimination Disorder | Sensory-Based Motor Disorder | |

| Sensory Over-Responsiveness | Sensory Under-Responsiveness | Sensory Seeker | | Postural Disorders | Dyspraxia |

Darwin
(Sensory Avoider)

Edward
(Sensory Disregarder)

Betsy & Filibuster
(Sensory Craver)

Andy
(Sensory Jumbler)

Carrie
(Sensory Slumper & Sensory Fumbler)

Chapter One

Darwin Goodenough, 11, Explains Sensory Processing Disorder

Are you an out-of-sync kid?

Me, too.

Here's what being out-of-sync feels like to me. I don't like it when someone nudges me or touches my hair. I'm choosy about clothes and food. My stomach gets upset when I move fast. I fall down a lot. Bright lights and loud sounds hurt my eyes and ears. I hate it when people think I'm not a good sport and say, "Don't be so touchy," and "Stop letting things bother you so much."

Is it that way with you, too?

Listen, lots of people I know are out of sync. My brother and sister, and even my parents are out of sync.

Our dog, Filibuster, gets out of sync, too. When he really needs to move, he goes wild and barks like crazy and tries to run outside. It's OK if he goes out the kitchen door to the back porch and yard because he is safe inside the fence. But once he slipped out the front screen door and ran into the street to chase cars. That was **not OK**. He almost got run over. Ever since, we always try to keep the front door closed tightly, because Filibuster has no street sense.

Anyway, the good thing is that our family mostly has good sense, and we work and play hard to get back in sync. Here's a story to show you how we do it. Everyone in my family is going to tell part of the story. My chapters are the longest because I talk the most, and besides, I have a lot of very important things to tell you. When you are done reading this book, maybe you and your family will have some good new ideas about getting in sync.

The story itself is short and is in big font like this. It is OK if you just read the story and look at the pictures.

> Information about what being out-of-sync is all about is in small font like this. You can read this information as you go along, or come back to it later when you are ready.

OK, let's go.

Do you have a good-luck charm? I do. Mine is a rabbit's foot on a key chain. Yesterday Filibuster ran off with it. He is usually a very good dog but was very bad yesterday. I freaked out, because what he did was **not OK**.

> When **not OK** things happen, I have a meltdown, or what Mom calls a FIDDLE Response.
>
> Now, I need to explain what FIDDLE means. In our family, FIDDLE is a word that means three different things.

1) One meaning is to fidget, like when your fingers play with a rabbit's foot.

2) The second meaning is a string instrument, usually a violin. Guess what? I play a big violin called a "violoncello," or "cello" for short. (Say, "CHEL-lo.") I like to practice musical scales. My cello teacher wishes his other students liked scales as much as I do, but most kids think scales are boring. I like them because they are orderly. You always know how each note fits with the others. You know what came before and what comes next and exactly where you stand.

When I practice, it is very, very important to me to stick to a routine. I need to do things my own way. And it is also very important to finish what I start. I try not to get upset when things don't go my way or when I'm interrupted, but it's hard. Do you feel that way, too?

I have perfect pitch. That means when I hear a note, I know that it is E flat or C sharp, for instance. Not many people in the world have perfect pitch, but a lot of extra sensitive people do, like me. Dad says it's one of the things that makes me special.

What I like best about the cello is that it sounds like what you're feeling. When I'm sad, the cello sounds sad. Or mad, or glad.

I also like to feel the vibrations coming through the strings and wood. Filibuster does, too. When I practice, he lies near my feet. He understands my feelings better than anyone, even better than Mom.

3) FIDDLE has a third meaning. Each letter in the word stands for an aspect of a meltdown. **FIDDLE** stands for…

F = Frequency (how often something happens), because I melt down a few times every day

I = Intensity (how strong something is) because my reponses to sensations are very strong, negative, emotional, and usually loud

D = Duration (how long something lasts) because my responses go on and on for a long time, sometimes hours or all day

D = Degree (how far something goes) because my response is "off the scale," or way beyond other people's responses to the same situation

L = Loneliness (how all alone you feel) because I feel as if no one really understands what it's like to be falling apart and out of control

E = Exhaustion (how used up and emptied out you feel) because a meltdown takes so much energy

Listen, I can't help having meltdowns. I have one when something really bothers me, and everything bothers me. So I need my rabbit's foot. I keep it handy and grab it and hold it tight whenever I'm uncomfortable. For instance, at school, when we're lining up for lunch, if somebody touches me and I don't expect it, I feel like I'm being hurt. The touch feels like a burn or a bee sting.

When that happens, I react right away with a *fight, flight, freeze, or fright response.*[1]

Sometimes a surprise touch makes me fight, and then everyone says I'm a troublemaker, even though it isn't ever my fault. Sometimes a surprise touch makes me run away, or "take flight," like a dumb dodo bird, and then everyone says I'm a sissy. Sometimes I freeze and can't move or talk and just stand there frozen to the spot. I don't know what everyone says about that, but I probably wouldn't like it. Sometimes I feel so scared that I cry. Then everybody laughs at me, and that is the worst.

I need my rabbit's foot then, because it's like my only friend, you know what I mean? I squeeze it, and it helps me relax. I need it at other times, too, like doing errands with Mom, because riding in the car makes me want to throw up.

The rabbit's foot is my favorite thing to fiddle with. It makes me feel calm and almost ready to try something that is usually **not OK** for me. See, if the tag in my shirt is itchy, or the orange juice has pulp, or the door has screechy hinges, see, those sensations are **not OK**. I need to close my eyes,

---

1. **Fight, flight, freeze, or fright response**: An instinctive reaction to defend yourself from real or imagined danger by withdrawing or becoming aggressive

breathe through my nose, do a few knee bends, and squeeze my rabbit's foot, and then I'll feel better.

OK, OK, I'm getting to the story, but first I have to tell you why some sensations make me over-react. I have a problem processing sensations. This problem goes by a bunch of different names. These days, lots of people use *Sensory Processing Disorder*,[2] or SPD.

The very smart woman, Dr. A. Jean Ayres,[3] who figured out the problem, called it Sensory Integration Dysfunction. Integration is the word for senses fitting and working together, deep inside your brain. You may hear therapists, doctors or teachers use the terms Sensory Integration Dysfunction, SI Dysfunction, Dysfunction in Sensory Integration, or DSI.

Whatever name you hear, the problem is the same. I wish there was just one name so nobody gets confused, but Mom reminds me that lots of things have more than one name, like pasta and macaroni, or P.E. and gym, or Mom and Betsy. It all depends on who's talking.

Anyway, we use Sensory Processing Disorder. "Sensory" has to do with the senses. "Processing" has to do with how the brain takes in, interprets, and uses sensory messages coming from

---

2. **Sensory Processing Disorder (SPD), or Sensory Integration Dysfunction, or SI Dysfunction, or Dysfunction in Sensory Integration, or DSI**: A problem in how your brain interprets sensory messages from inside and outside your body, making it hard to use sensations to keep safe, interact, and learn.

3. Ayres, A. Jean (1979). *Sensory Integration and the Child*. Los Angeles: Western Psychological Services.

inside and outside your body. "Disorder" in this case means a disturbance in the way your brain handles sensory information, causing problems with minute-to-minute daily living.

Defining this problem and giving it a name helps identify people who have it. Then therapists can give them lots of sensible ideas to help them be more comfortable and function better in their daily activities.

Sensory processing disorder is not contagious. If you come over to our house, don't worry, you can't catch it. It tends to be something you have in your family. My parents, my brother, my sister, and I have different types of this *neurological*[4] problem that happens in the brain.

Having a sensory processing problem doesn't mean you are dumb, but sometimes it feels that way to me and probably to you, too. We can be very smart and still have a hard time making sense of our senses.

We have seven senses. The five senses you already know about are seeing, hearing, smelling, tasting, and touching. They are sometimes called outer senses, because your eyes, ears, nose, mouth, and skin are on the surface of your body.

I need to tell you something about the sense of touch, or the *tactile sense*.[5] This sense tells you how things feel when they

---

4. **Neurological:** Having to do with the nerves and the nervous system.

5. **Tactile sense:** The sensory system that gives information received through your skin and hair about touch, pressure, vibration, movement, temperature, and pain.

touch your skin or hair. It gives you information about the texture, shape, size, and weight of things when you reach out and handle them. It tells you whether you are touching your Mom's warm hand; or a smooth, round doorknob; or a flat, dry book; or a slithery, slimy worm.

Your tactile sense also gives very important information about whether touch sensations are OK or **not OK**. For instance, an OK touch may be when you wrap a soft blanket around you. A **not OK** touch is when you are standing in line minding your own business and the kid next to you breathes on you.

We have two other senses, which are called the inner senses because they work inside your body. These are the vestibular ("ves-TIB-yoo-ler") and proprioceptive ("pro-pree-o-SEP-tiv") senses.

The *vestibular sense*[6] tells you where up and down are in relation to where you are. It tells you if you are lying down, balancing on one foot, spinning, falling, or bending over to tie your shoes. It tells you if you are moving, in what direction, and how fast.

Information about the pull of gravity and your own movement through space comes into a little vestibule, or entrance, to your inner ear. Little bones and membranes in there sense every move you make and tell you if the next move is good and safe or a really bad idea. When you tip your head, even a tiny bit, your vestibular sense tells you that you are off balance. You need this information so you don't fall.

---

6. **Vestibular sense**: The sensory system that gives information received through the inner ear about changes in head position and the pull of gravity.

You can't protect yourself when you're falling. You protect yourself best when your head is up, and you can hear with both ears and see with both eyes. You need to have both hands ready to grab hold of something or to catch yourself if you fall. Your vestibular sense keeps you upright and centered.

Another important inner sense is the *proprioceptive sense.*[7] This is the muscle sense, or the sense of body position. Every time you stretch or tighen a muscle, like curling your arm to make a big bicep, you get proprioceptive messages.

Proprioception lets you know where your hands and legs and other body parts are, even when you can't see them. It lets

---

7. **Proprioceptive sense**: The sensory system that gives information received through your muscles about where your body parts are and what they are doing.

you use just the right force to do things like pump air into a bicycle tire, kick a ball, and write without breaking your pencil point. It also lets you do things without looking at every little move your body makes, like sitting down in a chair, putting your arms into sleeves, buttoning your jacket, pedaling a bike, blowing bubbles, and going upstairs. Proprioception is like "internal eyes."

You know what it feels like when you don't have good proprioception? Your body feels sort of numb, the way your mouth feels when you get a shot of Novocain at the dentist's.

All your senses need to cooperate so you can do what you need to do, all day long. When one sensory system does not work—when it has dysfunction, or difficulty functioning—the other sensory systems don't have the support they need and so they have to work harder. All the senses should work smoothly together for a person to feel in sync.

Everyone has a problem processing sensations now and then. Scratchy wool fabric, spicy food, wind, seasickness, spinning, screechy brakes, and pins-and-needles when you hit your funny bone are things that bother lots of people. Usually, though, the problem isn't frequent or big enough to get in the way of moving, touching, playing, working, doing homework, talking to people, sleeping, waking up, going to school, eating, pooping, and other everyday sorts of jobs.

Around five or ten people out of every 100, including me, have problems with sensations many times a day. When something bothers us, we feel out-of-sync with the world and can't "just get over it." So, our job is to recognize the problem and work harder than most people to figure out what to do, or what not to do, so we can get through the day.

There are several different types and subtypes of sensory processing problems. (Look at the chart on page 5.) You could have just one type, or several of them.

You could have days when your sensory problems do not bother you at all. You could have days when your sensory problems really get in your way because you are tired, you stubbed your toe, recess was cancelled because of rain, your Mom forgot to put a note in your lunch, or you don't like your substitute teacher.

You could have days when your sensory problems really get in your way, and you will never know the reason. Are you surprised about all the variations? Do not be surprised.

Sensory processing disorder plays out differently in everybody, because everybody is different, and the combinations are endless. The way you respond to a situation depends on what happened before, what might come next, whom you're playing with, where you are, what you're thinking about, what time it is, what you ate for breakfast, how your socks feel, and on and on and on.

You know how you can take a few musical notes and combine them in lots of different ways to compose different songs? I'll show you. Here's a list of songs you probably sang when you were a little kid. Just sing these words, not the whole song:

Can you hear it? All you need is just three notes to sing five completely different tunes! I think that is so cool.

Well, the types of sensory problems are like musical notes. You can combine them in lots of ways, too, and come up with lots of different "tunes" for a situation.

Anyway, the type I have is a problem regulating, or modulating, my responses to sensations. Most people take in sensations and make what is called an *adaptive response*,[8] which is the obvious and best thing to do.

But when I take in sensations, my brain can't modulate them well. When someone taps me from behind, or my hands touch

8. **Adaptive response**: A change in the way you do something to meet a sensory challenge in the most useful way.

glue, or my mouth touches cucumber seeds, I feel overloaded and have a FIDDLE response. Another term for that is an *aversive response*.[9] That's how Mom explains to my teacher what happens to me.

My main problem is called *Sensory Modulation Disorder*.[10]

Sensory Modulation Disorder has three subtypes, or patterns. My pattern is *Sensory Over-responsivity*.[11] (My brother and Mom have different patterns.)

Sensory over-responsivity means that I pay so much attention to all kinds of sensations, even though I don't want to, that they get in my way. I always feel like I automatically need to defend myself. Sensory over-responsivity is also called sensory defensiveness.

Touch, movement, sights, and sounds bother me big-time. One of my problems is over-responsivity to touch sensations, especially surprise touches. This problem is called *tactile defensiveness*.[12]

---

9. **Aversive response**: A feeling of dislike or discomfort about a sensation and a strong wish to get away from it.

10. **Sensory modulation disorder**: A problem in your brain that makes it hard for you to adjust your responses to sensory messages so that the responses are "just right."

11. **Sensory over-responsivity**: Over-sensitivity to sensory stimulation, causing you to respond too soon, too much, and too often to ordinary sensations, as if they were painful or dangerous. You may seem negative and stubborn, or you may avoid interacting with people and things.

12. **Tactile defensiveness**: The type of sensory over-responsivity that causes you to react negatively and emotionally to unexpected, light touch.

For a typical kid, here's what happens. Say someone gives him a section of an orange. He touches it. It's soft, damp, and a little bumpy. It looks, feels, and smells OK, so he picks it up and eats it.

For me, here's what happens. When I touch the orange, my eyes tell me it's an orange, and I know it is something lots of folks like to eat. I like the smell but not the feel. My mouth doesn't want to touch it, either.

So instead of feeling OK about touching some ordinary things like an orange, I may get irritated at first. Then, if I can't get away from it, I begin to get annoyed. Then really annoyed, then aggravated, then upset, then angry!

Over-responsivity to movement, or *vestibular over-responsivity*,[13] is a problem, too.

I'm very cautious and don't like being pushed or moved. I hate escalators and elevators. I avoid merry-go-rounds and tire swings, because they make me seasick. Moving under my own steam is OK, but not too fast.

Another vestibular problem is the worry that I'm going to fall. This is *gravitational insecurity*,[14] sometimes called G.I. for short. Getting out of bed can be scary. Walking down stairs

---

13. **Vestibular over-responsivity**: A strong, negative, and emotional reaction to moving quickly or to spinning.

14. **Gravitational insecurity (GI)**: The extreme fear and anxiety that you will fall when you do not know where your head is in space, like when your feet leave the ground or your eyes are closed.

is scary, especially without banisters to hold, like outside the public library. Me get on the playground equipment? No way! My feet never leave the ground, because the possibility of falling makes me afraid.

Also, I have *visual defensiveness*.[15] Certain stimulation bothers me, like sunshine coming through Venetian blinds, or quick movement. I have to squint or cover my eyes or pull my baseball cap visor down to shut out distracting sights.

At recess, I get confused when the other kids shout and run around. My sense of *vision*[16] doesn't always process whether I'm moving or another kid is moving, so it's hard to make an adaptive response and get out of the way.

I don't move around like the other kids, but I do shout, especially when everyone else is noisy. Have you noticed what happens when you make your own noise? You don't hear anybody else! Certain sounds like loud voices or fire alarms hurt my ears because, guess what, I have *auditory defensiveness*.[17]

In fact, I'm over-responsive to every kind of sensation. The taste of vegetables, spices, mustard, licorice, and lots of other foods is gross. Smells bother me, too. When I was little, I cried when I smelled bananas or turpentine or people who

---

15. **Visual defensiveness**: Over-responsivity to bright lights and other distractions that you see.

16. **Vision**: The process of understanding what the eyes see and helping get ready for a response.

17. **Auditory defensiveness**: Over-responsivity to certain sounds like loud voices, sirens, fire alarms, slamming doors, radio static, and twanging metal guitar strings.

didn't wash their armpits. Now I don't cry, but I still hate certain smells and have learned to grab hold of my rabbit's foot and get away.

So, what does being over-responsive to sensations mean about my daily life? It means that getting through the school day takes so much work. So many things worry me. I get nervous when kids move in close because I am afraid they will touch me or knock me down. I need to stand against a wall, so I can see what's coming at me and be ready to defend myself before they get me.

Learning stuff is cool—I love reading, writing, math, science, music, and history—but school itself is **not OK** and wears me out. I wish I could just stay home and read, write, and play the cello, but Mom and Dad say then I wouldn't have friends.

I already don't have friends, so I don't see what difference it would make. But I guess they're right. Even if I think my family is good enough company, I suppose having a couple of friends would be nice, too.

On top of everything else, my sensory problems are worse if I don't get enough sleep or exercise. Then touching and being touched, and moving and being moved make me so uncomfortable I could pop out of my skin. When I'm overloaded with sensations, I don't function well, so I try to have as few sensations as I can. A person like me is a *sensory avoider*.[18]

My brother Edward is the opposite. He has another pattern of Sensory Modulation Disorder called *Sensory Under-Responsivity*.[19]

Edward is a *sensory disregarder*.[20] He is going to tell you about what that feels like in chapter three.

Mom says Edward and I are two sides of the same coin. Lots of times, something will annoy me but won't bother Edward at all. Or opposites will make us feel good. I like soft radio music, but Edward comes alive when it is loud.

---

18. **Sensory avoider**: Someone who withdraws from sensations.

19. **Sensory under-responsivity**: Under-sensitivity to sensations, causing you not to notice them very much. Sometimes you respond too late or not at all. You may pull away from life around you and may be hard to talk to and play with, or you may daydream all day.

20. **Sensory disregarder**: Someone who does not notice sensations.

My clothes have to feel just right, and Edward doesn't care what he wears. Actually, if his clothes fell to pieces, he probably wouldn't even notice.

Mom, Dad, and Carrie have different sensory processing problems. Keep reading, and you will find out that Mom is a sensory craver, Dad is a sensory fumbler, and Carrie is a sensory slumper. Everyone in our family has different needs because sensory problems play out differently in every person. The good thing is that *Occupational Therapy*[21] helps us all.

Mom and Dad get OT now and then, and we kids get it twice a week. OT is not just for grown-ups! It also helps kids do everyday activities and function smoothly, so we can do our job better. Our job, or occupation, is to play, learn, talk, eat, sleep, and have a good time being kids.

Grace is our Occupational Therapist. We started going to her clinic this summer and wish we had known her forever. She explains everything to us, so we understand why we feel the way we do and why the activities she suggests will help. She told us that at in graduate school, she got really

---

21. **Occupational Therapy (OT):** The use of specific activities to help people learn or relearn activities of daily living, like brushing hair or teeth, that give them problems caused by accidents, illness, learning disabilities, or sensory processing.

excited learning about sensory integration theory, which Dr. A. Jean Ayres developed in the 20th century. Dr. Ayres was a brilliant Occupational Therapist. Her theory made sense to Grace, and now she provides Occupational Therapy using a Sensory Integration framework, called OT/SI.

Grace gives us great ideas to do at home for a balanced *Sensory Diet*.[22] Most people satisfy their sensory systems by touching, moving, and interacting with people and things during the day, but people with sensory processing problems need help. You can read about our Sensory Diets in the Appendix in the back of this book.

Sensory Diet activities help us get ready to move from one situation to another. For instance, they help us get moving in the morning, go to school, come home, go to a friend's house or a birthday party, brush our teeth and hair, and go to bed.

The activities that a therapist suggests are specific for each person's individual needs. Often, *Heavy Work Activities*[23] are included, because they get you moving and feed your brain with tactile and proprioceptive messages.

This summer we dug a big hole in the backyard and imbedded a trampoline in the ground. If we fall off the trampoline, we don't fall far, just on the grass. Man, digging that hole was a lot of work! Dad says it was the best Heavy Work Activity ever.

---

22. **Sensory Diet**: A scheduled plan of multi-sensory experiences that an Occupational Therapist develops to help you become more self-regulated and in sync. A Sensory Diet may include activities that are alerting, organizing, and calming.

23. **Heavy Work Activities**: Jobs like carrying, pushing, pulling, and lifting heavy items; doing chores and yard work; and doing all kinds of vigorous physical work and play.

We do our Sensory Diet activities indoors and out. Indoor sessions in our basement gym are based on the sensory integration therapy we do with Grace. She wants us all to have fun together, and we sure do. We follow her suggestions every morning and sometimes at night, too. The more we do, the more Grace likes it. She says our Sensory Diet at home makes the work she does with us in her clinic much easier and gets us in sync quicker.

Go to the Appendix on page 65 to learn more about some Sensory Diet Activities that we like.

Chapter Two

Darwin Tells How Filibuster Nabbed His Rabbit's Foot

Yesterday was Labor Day. Since it was a holiday, we kids slept in.

Dad says sleep is important if we want to get in sync. He says that the amount of sleep that most kids get isn't good enough, but WE are Goodenough! (Get it? That's our last name. Dad is always saying stuff like that. It's so corny.) My sister Carrie and I should sleep eight or nine hours a day, and little kids like Edward should sleep 10.

After we got up, we ate breakfast.

Mom says protein for breakfast is another important part of getting in sync. You should see the things we get to choose for breakfast: granola, deviled eggs, pork and beans, sardines, tofu, and peanut butter. Something for everybody. Mom says it is not logical for anyone, especially growing children, to skip breakfast. Nobody in our family is allowed to skip breakfast. And you know what? Nobody in our family is fat, either. Do you know that eating a good breakfast makes you not so hungry for junk food during the day? That is a fact.

Dad says we need to drink a glass of water with every meal, and in-between meals, too. He says water is better than milk. Lots of people with sensory problems can't digest milk, cheese, yogurt, ice cream, and whatever else starts from milk. He is funny—he says that if we were calves, milk would be OK to drink, but we're people, so water is good enough for us. Did you know that a kid's body is about 65% water? That is a fact. So, of course, kids need to keep drinking water, or else they'll dry up.

After breakfast, the plan was to exercise in the basement. But the plan changed, and so we didn't start the day out right, and that's why we all ended up in the doghouse.

We have an awesome doghouse. It used to be Carrie's playhouse. When she got too tall to stand up inside, Filibuster moved in, and now it is his. Sometimes, when one of us needs to get away from it all, we crawl inside and rest. Usually, it's just one of us at a time, not like yesterday!

Here's what happened yesterday to change the plan. Dad got up early and went out to do errands while we slept. When we kids got up and saw he was gone, we decided to wait until he came home, because we love to play with him. Mom put on her headphones and went down to work out alone. She likes that every once in a while.

So, instead of doing Sensory Diet activities, I went to the living room to practice the cello. Edward went to the family room and got out his collection of Transformer® toys. Carrie went to her bedroom to do homework.

I took my cello out of the case and tuned it. I hung my rabbit's foot from the music stand and began practicing scales.

Filibuster circled three times, the way he does when he is restless and trying to settle down. When I began to play, he lay at my feet. The cello's vibrations calm him down.

Edward, though, doesn't appreciate my playing. In the other room, he started yelling. I ignored him.

Upstairs, Carrie began to scream. "I hate my hair!" she shouted. "And I hate those stupid scales! Stop, Darwin! And Edward, be gone!" She screamed and cried and banged things, and I was getting very irritated. I thought of fleeing to the back porch to crawl into the doghouse, but decided to fight her noise with my own noise. I played loud, angry, scratchy notes.

Then the screen door banged. And again. The hinges are rusty, and they screech. Now I was getting really aggravated and way out of sync. So I played louder and scratchier notes.

Filibuster was getting over-excited. His ears perked up, and he jumped to his feet. He ran in circles and growled so he could make his own noise and wouldn't have to listen to all of ours.

Then, oh, then, he nabbed my rabbit's foot.

Now everything was **not OK**. I was so upset. I put down my cello and tried to grab Filibuster, but I'm not good at catching things like skittering dogs. I tripped and fell against the piano bench and hurt my knee. I was very angry and out of control, and then I had a FIDDLE response, a big meltdown!

Mom came running up from the basement. She opened her arms. "Darwin, I'm right here. Give me a hug." Mom loves me so much. She squeezed me and rocked me slowly back and forth. After a while I began to calm down. She wanted to know what had happened, but I was a mess and could hardly talk. I managed to say that Filibuster got my rabbit's foot.

Then we went looking for Filibuster. We found him and the rabbit's foot, and everything turned out all right. We also found that we need to stick to our Sensory Diet routine every morning, if we expect to function in a good enough way!

Now everyone else in my family wants a turn to tell you their views of what happened yesterday to make us all end up in the doghouse. Edward is next.

> Oh, one more thing before I stop—you need to know that Edward cannot say sounds like "kuh" and "guh." Instead of "kuh," he says "tuh," and instead of "guh," he says "duh." So sometimes he will ask for a piece of chewing dum or birthday tate. He calls Carrie "Tarrie." It's OK with her. She's a nice big sister.
>
> We have a cousin named Cody, and Edward calls him Toady. Cody gets mad because he does not understand and thinks

Edward is doing it on purpose just to annoy him. I'll bet you know some people like Cody.

We do not tease Edward about the way he speaks because teasing does not help a person get better. Getting mad never helps, either. What does help is the right kind of therapy, like Occupational Therapy with Sensory Integration (OT/SI). Physical therapy and speech-and-language therapy along with SI are good, too. Lots of sensory-motor activities at home and school also help. Edward has speech therapy at school, and Grace helps him speak more clearly, too.

Don't worry. Like all of us in this family, Edward is working hard and getting better. I know you will not laugh at my brother. Here he comes now.

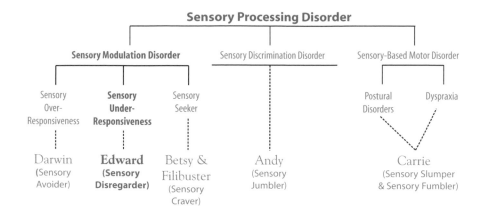

Sensory Processing Disorder

Sensory Modulation Disorder · Sensory Discrimination Disorder · Sensory-Based Motor Disorder

Sensory
Over-
Responsiveness

**Sensory
Under-
Responsiveness**

Sensory
Seeker

Postural
Disorders · Dyspraxia

Darwin
(Sensory
Avoider)

**Edward
(Sensory
Disregarder)**

Betsy &
Filibuster
(Sensory
Craver)

Andy
(Sensory
Jumbler)

Carrie
(Sensory Slumper
& Sensory Fumbler)

Chapter Three

Edward Goodenough, 5, Tells Why He Went Out the Front Door

Yesterday when Filibuster was being naughty, I was being sad. I wanted to watch TV, but Mommy said I would have to wait for my favorite show later. She says for a five-year-old, one hour is dood enough.

Oh, I am sorry. I should say, guh, guh, GOOD enough. "Guh" and "kuh" are so hard to say! I have therapy to learn how to say those sounds right, but my mouth still does it wrong. My tongue and lips do not have any sense at all. I have poor *oral-motor skills*.[24] That's what Drace—I mean GRACE—says.

At school, Miss Morrison helps me with speech. She is a speech therapist. I have auditory distrim… I mean, *auditory discrimination disorder*.[25] That means I don't process sounds very well. I don't always hear differences in sounds.

Miss Morrison is nice, but when I am with her, I have to miss recess, and that is so terrible. Everyone needs recess every day! If you don't move enough, you feel tired all the time.

---

24. **Oral-motor skills**: Movements of muscles in the mouth, lips, tongue, and jaw, affecting chewing, swallowing, and speaking.

25. **Auditory discrimination disorder**: The hearing and language skill of telling the differences between sounds, especially at the end of words.

I was lying in front of the TV, all zipped up in my Star Wars® sleeping bad. It was hot, but heavy weight feels nice.

I fiddled with my Transformers and lined them all up. I have nine. I love them so much. Once I hid them in bed, but Mommy found them and put them on the shelf. She was worried I would lie on them and hurt myself. But that wouldn't hurt me at all.

Then Tarrie—I mean kuh, kuh, CARRIE— started to yell. Then Darwin played terrible sounds. Then Filibuster made awful animal sounds in his throat. I heard it and sat up. Usually I don't notice things, but yesterday I sure noticed those loud sounds.

> Please do not be mad at me. Some people are mad when I do not notice things. After we paint, my art teacher is mad if I don't push up my shirt tuffs to wash up. She tells me to stop being lazy and to use my head. She is mean. She doesn't understand that I don't process the instructions well. I do the best I tan.
>
> Tarrie and Darwin are mad when I bump into things and they fall and brate. I mean BREAK. I do not do it on purpose. People tell me all the time to be tareful. They have to tell me, I suppose, 'tuz I do not pay dood enough attention to what I am doing. Do you know why? I have sensory under-responsivity.
>
> My brother has sensory over-responsivity. He is upset about every little tiny thing. But I am not. Unless it is a rumpus like what I'm telling you about.

Then Filibuster ran in the room. He had Darwin's rabbit's foot in his mouth. He was wild. He ran right into my Transformers and messed them all up. Now I was really paying attention, and I was mad! I yelled at him to stop, but he didn't listen.

I wanted Mommy, but she was not done in the basement, and we do not bother her unless it is really, really, really important. She says we have to leave her alone once in a while and try to solve our own problems.

I wondered where Daddy was. I went to the front door. Maybe he was out there.

I pushed open the streen door and went out. No Daddy in the front yard.

I went around to Filibuster's house. It is nice. It has windows and window botses with pretend flowers. Filibuster always lets us in. One of our Heavy Wort Attivities is to sweep it out so it smells nice.

Mommy and Daddy always have a zillion jobs for us. They say hard jobs help our muscles grow. Once I start moving, I want to move more. It is hard to start, though. I need help.

In his house, Filibuster has a really, really huge bed. Sometimes we pull it out of his house off the porch and into the yard. Pulling it is really hard. You feel your muscles all over your body. Then we line up and say, "Ready, Set, Doe!" I mean, "Ready, Set, GO!" Then we run and jump on to the bed. It is so fun. Mommy bought two more bed kuh, kuh, covers, and she washes them all the time so dawd hairs and fleas and stuff do not det up our noses.

The dawdhouse smelled a little bit of Filibuster, but I did not mind. I went in. I lay there in my sleeping bad on his bed. I put my thumb in my mouth.

Daddy says I am too old to sut my thumb, so I do it when nobody sees. At school, I chew on pencils instead. My thumb helps me think and feel better when I am out of synt. Daddy says I should chew dum, but yesterday all I had was my thumb. I needed it.

Then Filibuster ran up the porch steps and into the dawdhouse. His nose was all dirty, but I did not mind. I love everything about him. He slid inside my sleeping bad with me, and we hid.

I'm done telling you my part of the story. Here is my sister to tell you her part.

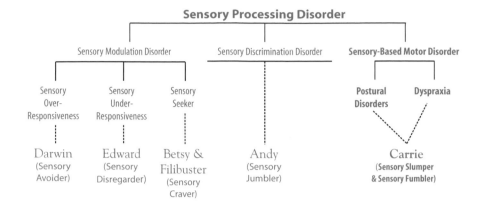

Sensory Processing Disorder

| Sensory Modulation Disorder | Sensory Discrimination Disorder | Sensory-Based Motor Disorder |

Sensory Over-Responsiveness | Sensory Under-Responsiveness | Sensory Seeker

Postural Disorders | **Dyspraxia**

Darwin
(Sensory Avoider)

Edward
(Sensory Disregarder)

Betsy & Filibuster
(Sensory Craver)

Andy
(Sensory Jumbler)

Carrie
(**Sensory Slumper & Sensory Fumbler**)

Chapter Four

Carrie Goodenough, 13, Tells About Having a Frizzy Fit

Good grief! What a mess we were all in yesterday! But we finally got in sync. Here's what happened. I was trying to write a short story for my first English assignment but got stuck. I didn't have any idea what to write about. I don't have a very good imagination, I guess.

So I went into the bathroom to brush my hair. I hoped that would make me alert and stimulate my writing skills. I knew I should have done Sensory Diet activities, but I wanted to wait for Dad.

Brushing my snarls was no easier than writing a little piece of fiction. It wore me out. I was already frustrated, and now I was about to have a frizzy fit.

Why I'm the only one in this family to be born with frizzy hair is beyond me. Brushing my hair is one of the most frustrating jobs. Getting dressed and riding a bike and even setting the table, which is pretty easy for girls my age, are all hard, too. When I try to do something new, like put on a new outfit, I put it on backwards, or stick my arms in the wrong sleeves. I have to do it at least 10 times before I do it smoothly. I'm always getting stuck.

Grace says I'm a *sensory fumbler*.[26]

She isn't trying to insult me. She just tries to help us kids understand why we have trouble doing things that seem so simple for other people.

Grace is a very positive and upbeat therapist. She wants us to be positive and upbeat, too. She wants us to be "in the know" about Sensory Processing Disorder. She says things like, "When you're in the know, you won't say no," and, "When you know why, then you will try."

Well, I try, and I try, and I try!

My brain isn't good at making sense of information I get about touch, movement, and body position to help me move in a coordinated way. Sensory information comes in to my brain all right, I notice it, and it doesn't bother or worry me, but using it to do things well just doesn't happen. I'm a huge klutz and sometimes doing something simple that I've done a million times before can be hard, like getting the brush through my dumb curls.

_____

26. **Sensory fumbler**: Someone who has difficulty using touch, movement, vision, and hearing messages to carry out a plan for a new, complicated action.

The type of Sensory Processing Disorder I have is *Sensory-Based Motor Disorder*.[27]

Sensory-Based Motor Disorder has two sub-types. I have both. Lucky me, ha ha ha! One sub-type is called *Dyspraxia*.[28] (Say, "dis-PRAX-ee-a.")

Dyspraxia means that I have mammoth problems getting started doing something new and complicated that I haven't done before, like, say, ice-skating or skipping stones across a pond or playing some song I just heard on the piano.

Some people, like my best friend Emily, don't have any trouble doing something new. For them, everything is a breeze.

The first time I went to Grace's clinic, I thought it looked like a fun place. But when Grace said to go ahead and play, I couldn't conceive of a single idea of what to do with a lot of the equipment and swings because they were new to me. One day, I brought Emily with me to therapy, and it was amazing all of the ideas she had when she saw the therapy rooms. She designed an obstacle course out of six pieces of equipment. We needed some help from Grace to put it all together, but Emily knew what to do to get started.

---

27. **Sensory-Based Motor Disorder:** Difficulty with movement and coordination caused by underlying sensory processing problems.

28. **Dyspraxia**: A problem in 1) conceiving of an idea for an unfamiliar action involving several steps, 2) putting the steps in order and figuring out a motor plan for how to do them, and 3) carrying out the plan.

Not me. I don't have the ideas yet, plus I'm awkward, accident-prone, and I have bad timing. I also have a problem with motor planning for *large-motor*[29] activities like kicking, for *fine-motor*[30] activities like cutting, and for oral-motor activities like chewing.

Having dyspraxia is so *dis*couraging, but Mom and Dad and Grace are so *en*couraging. When I get stuck and do the same things over and over again, like a car spinning its wheels in the mud, they help me think up new strategies to get unstuck.

Being in the know about dyspraxia improves my attitude. I now know I have to practice most new activities about 10 to 12 times before I get them. Other kids like Emily usually learn with a lot less practice than me, but at least I can count the tries and know I'm usually getting somewhere. I CAN do something to help myself, and I WILL.

Still, I seem to have one obstacle after another. As if dyspraxia weren't enough trouble, I also have *Postural Disorder*.[31]

This means that I'm sort of loose and floppy. I slump over my desk when I'm writing and twist my feet around the desk chair legs and have to remind myself to try to sit and stand up straight.

---

29. **Large-motor**: Having to do with movement of the big muscles in your arms, legs, and torso.

30. **Fine-motor:** Having to do with movement of the small muscles in your fingers, eyes, and mouth.

31. **Postural Disorder**: Difficulty with getting into and staying in a stable position without losing your balance, with keeping centered, and with moving your arms and legs together with smooth bilateral coordination.

Grace says I'm a *sensory slumper*,[32] but the movements that cause me trouble now will get easier with therapy, and I can't wait. For instance, it is hard to raise myself from a lying position to sitting without first rolling over onto all fours, because of a problem with *flexion*.[33]

Stretching my arms out to push a door open is hard, because of difficulty with *extension*.[34]

Going up and down stairs is not easy because of a problem with *weight shifting*.[35]

Turning to look left and right before crossing a street is uncoordinated because of difficulty with *rotation*.[36]

I'm terrible at sports. I have to work so hard, and I get so tired. In basketball, when I'm supposed to be dribbling the ball, mostly I'm just dribbling spit. I go to make a basket but can't keep both hands on the ball because I don't have good *bilateral coordination*.[37]

---

32. **Sensory slumper**: Someone who has difficulty with posture, balance, and bilateral coordination.

33. **Flexion:** Movement of the muscles around a joint to pull a body part toward its front or center. Bending.

34. **Extension:** The pull of the muscles away from the front of the body. Straightening or stretching.

35. **Weight shifting**: Moving the bulk of your body from one side to the other across the midline, as when throwing a ball or walking.

36. **Rotation**: Moving parts around your core, like swinging your arms or turning your head from one side to the other.

37. **Bilateral coordination**: Ability to use both sides of your body together smoothly and at the same time.

While I was tangling with my curls, Darwin began to practice his stupid scales, over and over again. BORRRR-ING. Why can't he just play tunes?

Now I got madder.

I started to cry and yanked the brush out of my hair, and that hurt a lot. Then I banged the brush on the sink, and the brush broke, and I yelled louder.

Downstairs, Edward started yelling, "Filibuster, you're a bad dawd!" And, "Darwin, be twi-et! Tarrie, be twi-et!"

> He meant to say, "bad dog" and "be quiet," but he can't when he is upset. He drools a lot, too. His therapists are working with him on his speech and language skills.

All of us were getting upset, and one person's reaction led to another person's reaction. Maybe that happens in your family, too.

I shouted, "Edward, be gone!" He must have been paying attention, because he stopped yelling. I heard him go out through the squeaky screen door.

Then Darwin played especially annoying sounds. They made me scream even louder.

Then Darwin had a meltdown. On a scale of 1 to 10, where 1 is good and 10 is terrible, his FIDDLE yesterday was an 8.5. (Remember what FIDDLE means in our family? See page 10.)

I couldn't stand it another minute. My mind went blank and I couldn't think of a new strategy. I needed some space. I got downstairs as fast as I could.

Because of dyspraxia, I have to go downstairs carefully so I don't trip and fall. "Left, right, left, right," I say to myself when I'm on the stairs or practicing drills for the marching band.

I know you won't believe it, but I actually am in the marching band at school. I play the snare drum. It was Dad's suggestion. He says playing an instrument makes me special. The drum is the only instrument I can play. Drumming helps me keep the beat, which is good, because I wasn't born with naturally good rhythm.

Maybe you wonder how people with sensory processing problems can do something complicated like play the drums or cello. People like us can play an instrument, or write their names beautifully or ride a bike, if they work very, very hard at mastering the skill. The skill they master is called a *splinter skill*.[38]

It's great to be good at something, but the problem is that a splinter skill doesn't help you learn other skills. I can play the snare drum because I practice like crazy, but could I play the glockenspiel? No way. At least, not yet.

---

38. **Splinter skill**: A particular ability that you work very hard to master but that does not help you learn more complicated tasks.

Drumming is fun but I get soooo mixed up with fancy footwork. I hear the bandleader say what we are supposed to do with our feet, but my feet don't get it unless I practice ten times more than everyone else. When I mess up, sometimes other kids laugh at me. I hate that, don't you?

Sometimes when I feel sorry for myself, I think that if I could just do the same-old, same-old things all the time, life would be so much easier.

I got downstairs and pushed open the screen door with a screech and a bang. I stomped outside, shoved open the garden gate, and marched up the porch steps to the doghouse.

Filibuster has the biggest, nicest doghouse in the world. When he is naughty, like when he grabs Edward's cookie, or "tuhtie," as Edward calls it, we shoo Filibuster out the kitchen door to his doghouse. We think it is funny to say, "Filibuster, you are in the doghouse!" He hangs his head and looks embarrassed, but we know he is happy to go out and get away from it all.

We all love to curl up inside the doghouse. We work to keep it clean. It's comfy and peaceful. It's our time-out place, but only when we want to be there, never because we are sent there. Mom and Dad feel that when we have a meltdown or frizzy hair crisis, we are not behaving that way on purpose. They know that sometimes we feel totally out of control. They know that the last thing to do with us when we are out of sync is to reject us and say, "You are in the doghouse!" The best thing to do is to say, "I'm here to help you. *I love you, no matter what.* How about a hug, for starters?"

You know, in our family, we don't use time out. Being sent to the corner doesn't make you feel better. It's much more helpful to figure out what is causing the problem and find a way to make things OK so the person with a sensory processing problem can feel included and join in. We call that time in.

When I got to the doghouse, was I surprised! Edward was already there. Filibuster, too.

"Can I come in?" I asked.

Filibuster wagged his tail.

Edward said, "O-tay." He scooted over and made room for me on the dog bed. The three of us lay there, side by side by side, until we were breathing in sync.

Now it's Mom's turn to tell you her part of this story.

Sensory Processing Disorder

Sensory Modulation Disorder | Sensory Discrimination Disorder | Sensory-Based Motor Disorder

Sensory Over-Responsiveness | Sensory Under-Responsiveness | **Sensory Seeker** | | Postural Disorders | Dyspraxia

Darwin
(Sensory Avoider) | Edward
(Sensory Disregarder) | **Betsy & Filibuster (Sensory Craver)** | Andy
(Sensory Jumbler) | Carrie
(Sensory Slumper & Sensory Fumbler)

Chapter Five

Betsy Goodenough, 39, Tells About Finding the Rabbit's Foot

It was good that yesterday was not a school day and we were home together, because Darwin was in a terrible state. I could hear him through my headphones while I was working out.

If I can just please count on an hour of vigorous exercise every day, I think I can handle almost anything. The type of sensory processing problem that I have is Sensory Modulation Disorder. My subtype is *Sensory Seeking*,[39] and I am a *sensory craver*.[40]

I need an immeasurable amount of sensory input. I'm always touching things, moving around, stretching, humming, and chewing. After Sensory Diet activities every morning and a long, pelting shower, I walk to the high school, where I teach math. I like doing hard work around the house, such as moving furniture, mowing, raking, and gardening. I'm constantly fiddling with a pencil, chalk, or rubber band. Always on the go!

---

39. **Sensory seeking**: An unquenchable need for strong, constant sensory stimulation.

40. **Sensory craver**: Someone who needs more sensory stimulation than others do to feel satisfied.

I ran upstairs and pulled my son into my arms.

Whenever Darwin has a FIDDLE response, I squeeze him tightly. I do not touch his hair or skin lightly, because light touch bothers him. Firm pressure is a thousand times better. It tells him, "Mom is here."

Then I had to figure out what had caused his meltdown.

You need to know the root of a problem before you can begin to solve it. For instance, we used to have a problem with family dinner. We are all picky eaters. Everybody has different likes and dislikes, so the formula for pleasing everyone was hard to find. When I realized that the problem was our sensory issues, life got easier.

Now, everyone has an assigned day of the week to choose what the family will eat. If you don't like what's on the menu, you have cereal and eat that with the family.

As a *sensory craver*, I like all kinds of flavors and textures in my food. The crunchier, the better! Granola bars, gum, beef jerky, apples, and celery give me good sensory stimulation in my mouth. Biting down on something hard actually helps me get organized and think clearly.

Andy, the Dad in our family, is a vegetarian. He doesn't eat meat, chicken, or fish, because of the bones. Once, he didn't notice that he had a fish bone in his mouth. He accidentally swallowed it, and it hurt his throat going down. He went to the hospital to get it out. His mouth can't always tell the difference between food that is chewable and safe to swallow, and things like bones or gristle that are not safe. He eats very carefully now.

Carrie has dyspraxia and so she likes easy food—easy to cut, easy to get to her mouth, and easy to chew. No grapefruit, lobster, or chicken wings for her!

Darwin, with sensory over-responsivity, prefers smooth food with no lumps, raisins, nuts, poppy seeds, or anything he calls "dots." His favorite food is hot dogs. On his night to choose the menu, the rest of us also have a side dish with texture, like carrots and celery, or spaghetti sauce, because his menus are too smooth and bland for the rest of us.

Edward, who has sensory under-responsivity, doesn't care what he eats, so on his night I make dinner as healthy as possible. I have to watch how much he eats because he doesn't stop, even when he should feel that he has had enough. He would keep eating infinitely. His sensory system doesn't tell him when he is full or hungry. It also doesn't tell him when he needs to go to the bathroom, but that is another story.

Analyzing the situation was hard because Darwin was totally irrational. Between sobs, he finally said, "Carrie screaming… door screeching… Filibuster stealing… rabbit's foot!"

This was not good. My son needs his rabbit's foot. It is like his security blanket.

I searched for the prime suspect. Where was that little dog? Where were Carrie and Edward? All gone—and the screen door was ajar! Filibuster must have escaped.

"Come on, Darwin. We have to find Filibuster. We can't let him run into the street."

Darwin and I went outside. He stood on the sidewalk, sobbing and helpless.

I reminded him, "What you need now is deep pressure to help you calm down. Cross your arms, squeeze your shoulders, and do a few squats. I'll be right back!"

Then I called, "Filibuster, Filibuster! Come home! We need you!" But Filibuster didn't come.

"Let's look around the house. Maybe he is in the yard." I stood behind Darwin and, pressing firmly on his shoulders, nudged him toward the back yard.

I noticed that the fence gate was open. I latched it behind us, and we went to the vegetable garden.

Well, guess what we found! An odd mound of fresh dirt between the tomatoes and peppers.

Hot diggity dog! This looked like Filibuster's work!

I poked around in the hole. Not surprisingly, I discovered the precious rabbit's foot. I held it up. "Ta-da! Darwin, look!"

Darwin began to sob again, this time with relief. "Mom, I love you!" he cried.

The rabbit's foot was spitty and covered with fresh dirt. Of course, Darwin wouldn't touch it. He began to sniffle again. When I told him that I would give it a bath, he rewarded me with a little smile.

One mystery solved, one child comforted. Next, I needed to find my other children to find out why Carrie was having a frizzy fit upstairs and to reassure Edward that I love him with all my heart and want him to be strong and active, and that is why I won't let him watch too much TV.

Maybe Carrie and Edward were on the swings or the trampoline. Darwin and I moved along to the back yard. No, they weren't there.

Then we went up the porch steps, and I'm sure you can guess what we found: Edward, Carrie, and Filibuster.

"There you are! Can we come in?" we asked.

"Sure!" Carrie said.

"Otay," Edward said.

"Woof!" Filibuster said, as he peeked out.

Darwin and I stooped down and moved inside.

Darwin looked at the dog sternly and said, "Filibuster, I don't like what you did! How would YOU like it if I took YOUR rabbit's foot?"

That was such a ridiculous idea, and Filibuster had such a perfect hangdog expression on his face, and we were so relieved that everything had calmed down, that we all burst out laughing. It felt good all over.

Then Andy came home and everything got even better. Now he will sum everything up and tell you how the day ended.

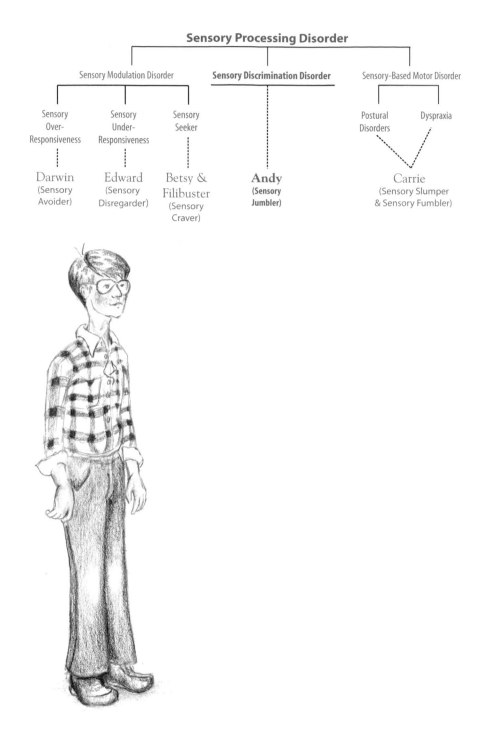

Sensory Processing Disorder

Sensory Modulation Disorder | **Sensory Discrimination Disorder** | Sensory-Based Motor Disorder

Sensory Over-Responsiveness | Sensory Under-Responsiveness | Sensory Seeker | | Postural Disorders | Dyspraxia

Darwin (Sensory Avoider) | Edward (Sensory Disregarder) | Betsy & Filibuster (Sensory Craver) | **Andy (Sensory Jumbler)** | Carrie (Sensory Slumper & Sensory Fumbler)

Chapter Six

Andy Goodenough, 41, Tells About His Family Getting Back in Sync

Labor Day morning, before the kids got up, I went to do errands. My plan was to be home soon to play together in the basement.

> All those Sensory Diet activities we do every day are good for everybody's constitution. I've noticed lately that Carrie's coordination is smoother, Darwin's meltdowns are briefer, and Edward has more energy and his speech is clearer. The more we move, the happier Betsy and I are, too.

First stop was the home and garden center. I needed a shovel for transplanting small trees and big bushes. The shovel I had been using was too flimsy. I'm glad I remembered to bring it into the store with me to make a comparison. Even then, when I held two shovels, it was hard to judge which was heavier.

> The reason that it is hard for me to sense the differences in how things weigh, look, sound, and feel is that I have the type of sensory processing problem called *Sensory Discrimination Disorder*.[41]

41. **Sensory Discrimination Disorder**: A problem interpreting differences between sensations.

I am a *sensory jumbler*[42] and don't feel subtle differences between things. Sometimes I don't sense obvious differences, either, even if they are right before my eyes or under my nose. Yesterday, I didn't notice that Betsy got a really short haircut until she stood right in front of me and asked, "Notice anything

42. **Sensory jumbler**: Someone who cannot easily judge how one sensation is different from a similar sensation.

different?" And to save my soul, I cannot tell by taste alone if the jelly in a PB&J sandwich is grape or strawberry.

I picked up a couple of possibilities and chose a shovel that looked right. It was a lucky guess.

I bought some large sacks of organic fertilizer. Unloading and spreading the fertilizer later would be a great Heavy Work activity for the kids. I'm a lucky Dad to have kids who actually enjoy being helpful.

From a display at the checkout counter, I also chose three rabbits' feet. Darwin's is so worn out that I thought treating him to a new one would make sense. Getting two more for Carrie and Edward seemed politically correct, too.

After loading up the car, I drove to the pet store for rawhide bones.

Betsy says Filibuster needs appropriate *oral-motor stimulation,*[43] so he'll stop chewing the kids' shoes.

In the store, I read all the labels carefully, so I wouldn't buy a dog toy with toxins. Some rawhide bones have preservatives, artificial color, and even caramel added. Who needs that? There were so many choices, and I couldn't be sure which was the kind Filibuster usually chews.

---

43. **Oral-motor stimulation**: Activities such as sucking, biting, crunching, chewing, and licking that provide sensory input to the mouth, lips, tongue, and jaw.

I bought some that had no additives and looked familiar. Outside the pet store, I wasted time looking for my car. Silver cars like mine are popular, and in a parking lot they all look alike to me, but I finally found it.

Now I was eager to get home to spend time with my family but made one more stop. At a roadside stand, I bought Betsy a bouquet of roses. Just because.

When I got home, I called for the kids to come help unload the fertilizer. Nobody answered. Where was everyone? I went around to the back yard to find my family.

When I went up the porch steps, here is what I saw: the whole family was in the doghouse!

"Hey!" I said.

"Andy! Dad! Daddy! Woof!" they said all at once.

I asked, "Got room for one more?"

"Sure!" they said. "We always have room for one more!"

I crawled into the doghouse, careful not to crack my head on the doorway, and we had a family squeeze. It felt just right, all over, like landing in a warm, safe place.

Then I distributed the rawhide, rabbits' feet, and roses, and felt that everyone was pleased. I polled the kids to see who wanted to do Sensory Diet activities, and they voted unanimously to start right away, so that is what we did.

Later, we unloaded the bags of fertilizer from the car and lugged them to the garden. It took no time at all to spread the fertilizer. Many hands make quick work.

We had a cookout with hot dogs, tofu burgers, and grilled vegetables, while Filibuster gnawed on his rawhide. As the sun went down, we sat on the porch talking about school, the up-coming Presidential election, cello and drum vibrations, Transformers, preservatives in dog toys, and Carrie's idea for writing a story about a naughty dog.

So the day ended, and the consensus was that we were all back in sync. We were functioning well and could get our work done, enjoy being together as a family, and have fun, too. All in all, good for the Goodenoughs!

Appendix

Darwin Describes Sensory Diet Activities

The Goodenough Family's Indoor Sensory Diet Activities

A few months ago, we set up some simple equipment in our basement. Every morning our whole family plays together for half an hour or more. We do specific activities that get us ready for the day. Here are some of the things we do. If you are interested in any of the equipment that I'm telling you about, see the list on page 75.

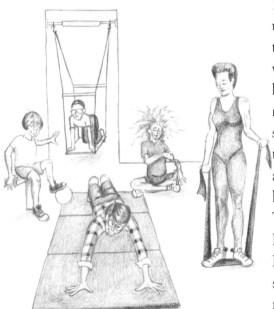

1) *Marching.* For about 15 minutes, we do different things to warm up. First, we march to music. I like Mozart, because his music is clear and makes so much sense. I listen to Mozart all the time, and it helps me with my homework. Edward likes Tom Chapin and Kidz Bop. Carrie likes John Philip Sousa, because she plays his music in the marching band. Mom

likes peppy music, like the Beatles, Def Leppard, and rock-and-roll oldies but goodies. Dad likes Stan Getz and all that jazz.

We take turns choosing the music. Even if I think everyone else's music is not good enough, I have to be nice about it. It's a Goodenough rule. (Get it? That's our last name. Dad is always saying stuff like that. It's so corny.)

2) The *Cross Crawl*. This warm-up movement is from a program called *Brain Gym.*®[44]

The Cross Crawl isn't really crawling. To do the Cross Crawl, you touch your right hand to your left knee, and then your left hand to your right knee. That's it, basically. Want to stand up and try it? You can do the Cross Crawl in other ways, too. Do the Cross Crawl while you skip. Raise your knees one at a time and touch them with the opposite elbows. Reach behind you to touch the opposite foot.

The Cross Crawl is good for *crossing the midline.*[45]

Crossing the midline helps the two sides of your brain "talk to each other." Then you feel more awake and have more energy.

---

44. **Brain Gym**: A movement system that helps integrate your senses of seeing, hearing, and moving.

45. **Crossing the midline**: Using one part of your body, such as your hand, foot, or eye, on the opposite side of the body, such as using your right hand in your left body space.

3) *Deep pressure to our arms, legs, and backs.* Next we get our tactile systems ready. We rub our arms and legs with lots of pressure, using paintbrushes, baby hairbrushes, and Teflon® pot scrubbers.

We use soft plastic corn silk brushes, too. Do you know what those are? They're for removing strands of yellow silk from corn on the cob. Mom brought them home from the grocery store and said, "We can add these to our deep pressure tools."

Dad laughed and said, "Capital idea! Much better than using them to remove corn silk. For that job, Goodenough fingers should be good enough!"

Our Mom and Dad are always coming up with new ways to use simple things as sensory tools. You don't need fancy equipment. Grace says most people have everything they need in "natural settings" like the kitchen and yard.

We also rub our skin with pieces of fabric—terry cloth, velvet, corduroy, fake fur, and burlap. Applying deep pressure with different things helps me be less aware of touches and helps Edward be more aware. Deep pressure is good for Dad to help him recognize how things feel. Sometimes we'll rub his back with a paintbrush or washcloth and ask him to guess what we have used. Deep pressure is good for Mom, because she is happy when she's touching and being touched, and it's good for Carrie because it helps her motor coordination.

4) *Doing push-ups.* Dad, Edward, and I do push-ups on our hands and knees. Mom does them with her feet resting on

a therapy ball. Carrie does them standing up and pushing against the wall.

5) *Doing pull-ups on a chinning bar.* Lifting your own weight is hard. It takes practice. I can do two pull-ups. My goal is eight. If you do pull-ups every day, your muscles will get stronger fast.

6) *Playing with stretchy bands.* We each take an exercise band and play a follow-the-leader game while we count out loud or listen to music. Pulling on a stretchy band is a resistive activity. It is very good for proprioception. Proprioceptive activities help everybody feel alert and ready. If you are fidgety or anxious, they calm you down. If you are sluggish and need a jumpstart, they get you up and running.

We kids love a game Mom plays with us called "Mummy Wrap." She stretches long exercise bands around us from shoulder to ankle. All that pressure against our skin feels great. Carrie likes to jump on the trampoline for extra sensory input. Edward and I like to waddle around and moan, like we're dead Pharaohs. Maybe it looks weird, but we think it's funny, and who cares, because it makes us feel better.

7) *Jumping on the mini-trampoline.* When we jump, usually Mom chants poems and claps her hands to keep the beat. Here's an example of a good jumping poem. Read it aloud. Clap your hands each time you see an accent mark, like this (´), on top of a word, and you will hear and feel the beat. Try jumping to it. We think it's fun.

> My fáther is a bútcher,
> My móther chops the méat,
> And I'm´ the little hót dog
> Who rúns around the stréet.

If you think the poem is immature for a boy my age, sorry. I have always liked it because hot dogs are on my list of OK Foods. Edward likes it, too. Not because of hot dogs, though. He wouldn't care if you changed "hot dog" to something gross like "ox-tail" or "liver." He likes the poem because the rhythm is strong and helps him with his ear-body coordination, so when he jumps, he's in sync.

8) *Using a therapy ball.* We have five therapy balls, all different sizes and colors. One is a Chair Ball that has little feet to keep the ball from rolling away when you stand up. Sitting on the ball is called dynamic sitting, because you constantly have to make adaptive responses so you don't fall off. I sit on one and bounce just a little bit. I usually keep my feet on the floor because of the problem I told you I have with gravitational insecurity. Grace is helping me to try new moves, and soon I'll be more comfortable bending and jiggling and letting my head get into different positions.

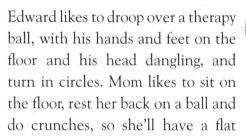

Edward likes to droop over a therapy ball, with his hands and feet on the floor and his head dangling, and turn in circles. Mom likes to sit on the floor, rest her back on a ball and do crunches, so she'll have a flat stomach. Carrie pretends the therapy ball is a movie star she is in love with and she hugs it. Dad presses it between his back and the wall and does squats. You can do a million different things with therapy balls, and they are all good for sensory processing.

9) *Balancing on a T-stool.* A T-stool is a stool that is shaped like, guess what, a "T" and has one leg. When you sit on a T-stool, you wobble, and Grace says that's good. Wobbling means you're using all your core muscles, especially in your stomach, back, and rear end, so you can stay upright and centered. Sitting on a T-stool is really fun. Believe it or not, it helps you pay attention and have better posture. Our T-stools are adjustable, so we can make them higher as we kids grow taller.

10) *Swinging.* Slowly moving forward and back or side to side is usually calming. Everybody's different, of course, so Grace makes sure we each have our own swinging activities that she suggests for our particular problem. We do it on suspended equipment. That's swings and stuff that occupational therapists hang from hooks in the ceiling at their clinics. At home, maybe you have suspended equipment, too, like a swing set in your backyard, or a tire swing hanging from a big tree branch. If you like swinging and do it a lot because it feels good, then you're doing self-therapy.

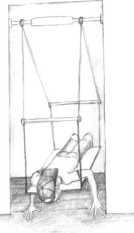

Indoors, your Mom or Dad can hang suspended equipment from a support bar, sort of like a chinning bar, that you can put up in a doorway. We have an indoor playground set that has swings, a glider, a ladder, a trapeze, a net swing, and a platform you can sit on, lie on, crouch on, or stand on.

We sit on the platform and throw beanbags into a basket. Or we lie on the platform and do the Fish Walk. We pretend we're floating near the bottom of the ocean and "walk" our hands on the ocean floor.

Mom and Dad like to hang out in the suspended equipment, too. Once, we were calling and calling Dad to come to supper, and he wasn't answering. Finally, we found him asleep in the net swing!

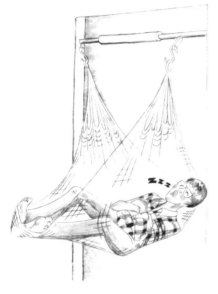

Swaying slowly on a swing or platform very close to the ground is called *linear movement*[46] because it goes in a straight line. Slow forward-and-back movement is organizing and relaxing. When the swing goes higher through space in a circular arc, it is *rotary movement*.[47] Rotary movement is stimulating.

Rotary movement, like high swinging or spinning in circles, is good for Edward. It wakes him up. In fact, when he gets on a spinning platform or tire swing, you can't get him off. He says, "I'm staying here for a million minutes." I hate rotary movement because it upsets my stomach. The minute the swing or platform begins to pick up speed, I want to get off. Grace is working with me so I can tolerate moving faster, highter, and in different

46. **Linear movement**: A motion in which you move in a straight line, from front to back, side to side, or up and down.

47. **Rotary movement**: Turning or spinning in circles, or moving through space in a circular way, such as on a merry-go-round, Ferris wheel, or high-flying swing.

directions. I'll be glad when moving starts feeling better. She promises it will.

11) *Rolling around on the floor.* I don't like rolling unless it is very slow and flat on the floor. Everybody else in my family thinks it is fun to pretend to be logs or pencils. Grace says I will, too, when my neurological system is ready.

12) *Playing "People Sandwich."* We pretend that a gym mat or mattress is a slice of sandwich bread. We lie on it, face down. We say that we are a sandwich filling like turkey, ham or peanut butter. Then someone, usually Mom, rubs make-believe mayonnaise and mustard down our backs and legs. She spreads this pretend goop with her hands or a sponge, or rolls it on with a big therapy ball. Then she lays another gym mat over us. That's the top slice of bread. Then she says, "Whoops! Too much mayonnaise! Got to squish some out!" She presses down on the mat really hard to get out the extra mayonnaise. Between the mats, inside the sandwich, we feel great. That's because deep pressure feels wonderful on your skin, muscles, and joints.

The Goodenough Family's Outdoor Sensory Diet Activities

We do other Sensory Diet activities outdoors, even in the winter. Mom and Dad insist, because fresh air and sunshine keep us healthy. Where we live, which happens to be Washington, DC, being in the winter sun for 15 minutes a day is good enough to give you the vitamin D you need to build strong bones. That is a fact.

Here are some of the things we do for our Sensory Diets out in the backyard:

- Edward spins on the tire swing.

- Carrie swings on the porch glider.

- Dad digs.

- Mom jumps on the big trampoline.

- Filibuster runs around. And sometimes, when he is very naughty, he digs a hole and buries something he is not supposed to have.

- I find a soft, quiet place like Filibuster's doghouse. I crawl in, curl up, rock slowly forward and back, and fiddle with my rabbit's foot.

Believe me, these activities are simple and they help everybody, with or without Sensory Processing Disorder, to get in sync. I can't wait for you to try them, because I just know you will feel good all over!

Equipment

A Chair Ball (like the one Darwin is using on page 70) has little peg feet that keep it from rolling away. You can also hold on to the feet while you bounce.

Henry Occupational Therapy Services, Inc.
P.O. Box 145, Youngtown, AZ 85363-0145
Phone & Fax: (623) 933-3821, Toll free: (888) 371-1204
e-mail: dianahenry@henryot.com
website: www.ateachabout.com

A Gym Mat (like the blue one that Andy is using on page 65) is a piece of equipment you can use indoors or outdoors for rolling, jumping, and somersaulting on and for playing People Sandwich.

Integrations
P.O. Box 620860, Atlanta, GA 30362
Phone·   Toll-free: (800) 622-0638
               International: (770) 449-5700
Fax: Toll-free: (800) 845-1535
               International: (770) 263-0897
e-mail: customer.service@sportime.com
               catalogrequest@sportime.com
website: www.integrationscatalog.com

The Rainy Day Indoor Playground (like the one Darwin is using on page 71) is innovative, educational, and developmentally sound equipment that turns any standard doorway into an energy-releasing, muscle-coordinating way to have fun. Interchangeable parts include swings, trapeze bar, glider, net swing, platform, and ladder. Requiring no tools to install, the set is portable and transportable from door to door or house to house.

A T-Stool (like the one Edward is using on page 65) is a one-legged seat that helps a person balance and stay upright. The leg is adjustable in height, so as the child grows, so does the chair.

Playaway Toy Company, Inc.
Mail: P.O. Box 247, Bear Creek, WI 54922
Phone: (715) 752-4565, or Toll free: (888) 752-9929
Fax: (715) 752-4476
e-mail: therapis@frontiernet.net
website: www.playawaytoy.com

Stretchy Bands (like the ones Darwin and Edward are using to play "Mummy Wrap" on page 68) are non-latex exercise bands that you pull on to get proprioceptive input into your muscles.

A Trampoline (like the big one the Goodenoughs installed in their back yard on page 38) gives you a good work-out when you jump on it and helps develop your vestibular system.

Abilitations
P.O. Box 620856, Atlanta, GA 303462
Phone: Toll free: (800) 850-8602
           International: (770) 449-5700
Fax: Toll free: (800) 845-1535
           Local or international: (770) 263-0897
e-mail: customer.service@sportime.com
           catalogrequest@sportime.com
website: www.abilitations.com

Helpful Websites

We have set up a family website for the Goodenoughs where you can read about their latest adventures, ask questions, share information, learn about research on sensory processing disorder, and find other sensory resources.

www.TheGoodenoughs.com

The KID Foundation sponsors an online site with lots of information about sensory processing disorder. There are all types of community and healthcare resources for people with sensory problems, including dentists; physicians; occupational, physical and speech-language therapists; educators; mental health professionals; and eye care professionals. The site is adding community resources, such as hair salons and gymnastics programs. If you know of resources in your area, please visit this website and add them to the list.

This site also includes a link to SPD Parent Connections, an nationwide network of parent-managed community support groups for families interested in sensory processing problems.

www.SPDnetwork.org

Carol Kranowitz has a website that includes many pages of equipment, supplies, and other resources to assist people with sensory processing disorder. It also includes links to other useful sites.

www.out-of-sync-child.com

S.I. Focus magazine is the first of its kind serving as an international resource to parents and professionals who want to stay informed about sensory integration and how to address sensory processing deficits. *S.I. Focus* provides quality information written by leading people in the field as well as parents with insight into the topic.

www.SIFocus.com

Sensory Resources, the publisher of this book, also publishes additional books, videos, CDs, audiocassettes, and other materials on sensory processing disorder and related topics. Sensory Resources sponsors workshops for parents, teachers, therapists, and others interested in sensory processing problems.

www.SensoryResources.com

Future Horizons is the world's largest publisher exclusively devoted to resources for those interested in autism spectrum disorders and Asperger's syndrome, many of whom also have sensory processing problems. If you have an interest in autism, please visit this site.

www.FutureHorizons-autism.com

The Terms We Use to Describe Sensory Processing Disorder

In 2004, a committee of Occupational Therapists clarified the terms we use to describe sensory problems. The committee included Lucy Jane Miller, PhD, OTR, FAOTA; Sharon A. Cermak, EdD, OTR/L, FAOTA; Shelly J. Lane, PhD, OTR/L, FAOTA; and Marie E. Anzalone, ScD, OTR, FAOTA; as well as Beth Osten, OTR; and Stanley I. Greenspan, MD.

The chart, which shows the various types of sensory processing problems, is the basis for the charts that appear at the front of each chapter to illustrate the types of sensory problems that affect the members of the Goodenough family.

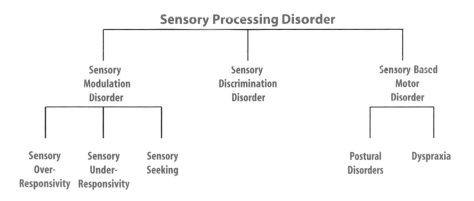

Glossary & Index

Dyspraxia: A problem in 1) conceiving of an idea for an un-familiar action involving several steps, 2) putting the steps in order and figuring out a motor plan for how to do them, and 3) carrying out the plan.   43, 44, 47, 53

Extension: The pull of the muscles away from the front of the body. Straightening or stretching.   45

FIDDLE: Acronym for Frequency, Intensity, Duration, Degree, Loneliness, Exhaustion.   8, 10, 20, 32, 46, 52

Fight, flight, freeze, or fright response: The instinctive reaction to defend yourself from real or imagined danger by with-drawing or becoming aggressive.   11

Fine-motor: Having to do with movement of the small muscles in your fingers, eyes, and mouth.   44

Flexion: Movement of the muscles around a joint to pull a body part toward its front or center. Bending.   45

Gravitational insecurity (GI): The extreme fear and anxiety that you will fall when you do not know where your head is in space, like when your feet leave the ground or your eyes are closed.   21, 69

Heavy Work Activities: Jobs like carrying, pushing, pulling, and lifting heavy items, doing chores and yard work, and doing all kinds of vigorous physical work and play.   26, 37, 61

Proprioception/Proprioceptive sense: The sensory system that gives information received through your muscles about where your body parts are and what they are doing.

Rotary movement: Turning or spinning in circles, or moving through space in a circular way, such as on a merry-go-round, Ferris wheel, or high-flying swing.

Rotation: Moving parts around your core, like swinging your arms or turning your head from one side to the other.

Self-therapy: Active, willing participation in experiences that help you feel in sync, because they help you respond to sensory stimulation, such as spinning in circles to stimulate your vestibular sense.

Sensory avoider: Someone who withdraws from sensations.

Sensory-Based Motor Disorder: Difficulty with movement and coordination caused by underlying sensory processing problems.

Sensory craver: Someone who needs more sensory stimulation than others do to feel satisfied.

Sensory Diet: The multi-sensory experiences that you usually seek every day to satisfy your sensory appetite. A Sensory Diet is also an activity program that an Occupational Therapist develops to help you become more self-regulated and in sync.

Building Bridges through Sensory Integration

by Ellen Yack, Shirley Sutton, and Paula Aquilla

Book

$**34**.95

New US Edition! Perfect for those working with young children, but broad enough to be adapted for older children and adults. Three experienced occupational therapists wrote this must-have practical guide for professionals, parents, teachers, and caregivers.

Provides many creative techniques and useful tips while offering innovative strategies and practical advice for dealing with everyday challenges. Includes strategies for managing behaviors, improving muscle tone, developing social skills, creating sensory diets—and more!

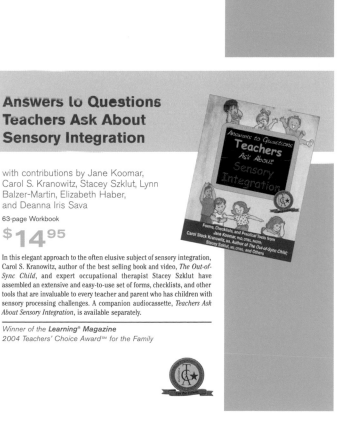

Answers to Questions Teachers Ask About Sensory Integration

with contributions by Jane Koomar, Carol S. Kranowitz, Stacey Szklut, Lynn Balzer-Martin, Elizabeth Haber, and Deanna Iris Sava

63-page Workbook

$**14**.95

In this elegant approach to the often elusive subject of sensory integration, Carol S. Kranowitz, author of the best selling book and video, *The Out-of-Sync Child*, and expert occupational therapist Stacey Szklut have assembled an extensive and easy-to-use set of forms, checklists, and other tools that are invaluable to every teacher and parent who has children with sensory processing challenges. A companion audiocassette, *Teachers Ask About Sensory Integration*, is available separately.

*Winner of the **Learning**® Magazine*
2004 Teachers' Choice Award℠ for the Family

Preschool Sensory Scan for Educators
(Preschool SENSE)

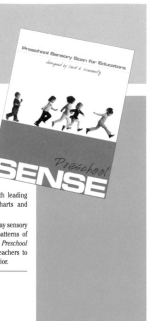

designed by Carol S. Kranowitz, author of *The Out-of-Sync Child*

Workbook

$9⁹⁵

A valuable new collaborative tool that occupational therapists can share with teachers who are striving to help preschoolers with sensory processing disorders. Developed by best-selling author and preschool teacher Carol Kranowitz in consultation with leading occupational therapists, this handy tool includes easy-to-use charts and checklists that fit the busy preschool classroom and playground.

With side-by-side examples of typical and atypical responses to everyday sensory stimuli, this program helps teachers to recognize the emerging patterns of sensory processing disorder among their most challenging students. *Preschool SENSE* is a great way for occupational therapists and preschool teachers to collaborate on simple accommodations that address out-of-sync behavior.

Available Fall 2004!

Danceland

with musical host Aubrey Lande

CD (51 min.) & 32-page Booklet

$21⁹⁵

Audiocassette (51 min.) & 32-page Booklet

$19⁹⁵

Fly aboard an imaginary airplane to the "exotic continent of musicality," exploring all the sensory-motor activities hidden in *Danceland*. Polka to an authentic Krakowiak or have kids choreograph their own movements to singer Laura Dart's "Touch the Earth." Kids can croon karaoke-style to an uproarious re-make of the 60's hit "Wild Thing" or have a Kwanzaa party to "Wisdom of Africa." Includes a 32-page Travel Guide, written by developmental dance specialists, that contains safe, sound activities for all ages and abilities.

Danceland opens up the taste buds of your ears. Join in for a worldwide adventure in music and movement.

— Don Campbell,
author of *The Mozart Effect*

These products are available from www.SensoryResources.com or by calling 888-357-5867

I Like Birthdays...
**It's the Parties
I'm Not Sure About!**

by Laurie Renke; illustrated by
Jake Renke and Max Renke

Book

$**14**⁹⁵

A wonderful new children's book about birthdays! Have
you ever noticed how many children are bothered by the loud "Pop!" of a
balloon? Read this book to understand why some children don't like parties.
Learn to understand what a child's actions are really saying and learn about
sensory processing disorder through the eyes of a child.

Coming Soon—Available Fall 2004!

The Sensory Connection

by Nancy Kashman
and Janet Mora

Book

$**24**⁹⁵

Provides practical advice and workable strategies to treat
dysfunction in sensory integration and communication
disorders through a team approach.

Drawing on their extensive experience in developing and implementing
effective treatment strategies in clinical, school, and family settings, Nancy
and Janet demonstrate how an integrated team approach increases
therapeutic effectiveness while maximizing the benefits of the available
treatment resources.

These talented and experienced therapists explain how to develop more
effective treatments within the resource constraints that therapists often
face. They include development of child-centric strategies that combine
aspects of occupational and speech-language therapies.

I heartily recommend this book!

— Georgia DeGangi, Ph.D., author of
*Pediatric Disorders of Regulation
in Affect and Behavior*

New! Available Fall 2004

These products are available from www.SensoryResources.com or by calling 888-357-5867

W9-BGD-54

GREATEST MOVIE MONSTERS™

DRACULA
AND OTHER VAMPIRES

HEATHER MOORE NIVER

rosen publishing's
rosen central®

Published in 2016 by The Rosen Publishing Group, Inc.
29 East 21st Street, New York, NY 10010

Copyright © 2016 by The Rosen Publishing Group, Inc.

First Edition

Library of Congress Cataloging-in-Publication Data

Niver, Heather Moore.
Dracula and other vampires/Heather Moore Niver.—First edition.
    pages cm.—(Greatest movie monsters)
Includes bibliographical references and index.
ISBN 978-1-4994-3525-2 (library bound)—ISBN 978-1-4994-3526-9 (pbk.)—ISBN 978-1-4994-3527-6 (6-pack)
1. Vampire films—History and criticism—Juvenile literature. I. Title.
PN1995.9.V3N57 2015
791.43'675—dc23

2014046124

Manufactured in the United States of America

On the cover: Christopher Lee stars in "Horror of Dracula," 1958.

CONTENTS

CHAPTER 1

THE VERY FIRST VAMPIRES

The word *vampire* may summon up images of a cold, dark castle, deep in the distant countryside of Hungary, and a black-caped figure who lurks in the shadows, with pale skin and a pair of bared white fangs. But this description of a vampire was popularized by one author—Bram Stoker. Before him, there were many vampire stories with a diverse cast of creatures, but all with one familiar trait: a lust for blood.

MYTHS, LEGENDS, AND LORE

Vampire stories have been around for thousands of years, though the word *vampire* became popular only in the seventeenth and eighteenth centuries. Traditionally, vampires are created by being bitten by another vampire, but other methods have been suggested, such as witchcraft and—believe it or not—a cat jumping over a corpse. Count Dracula, the vampire in Bram Stoker's novel *Dracula* (1897), popularized the vampire genre and created a vampire type with some basic similarities. Mysteriously brought back to life after death, vampires, also known as the undead, rise at night from the grave or a coffin filled with the soil of their native country. Under the cover of darkness, these gruesome (or gorgeous, depending on the story-teller) creatures feed on human blood. Stoker-type vampires also do not make a shadow or have a reflection.

Bela Lugosi (shown here with Elizabeth Allan) played the character of Dracula as a mysterious, sexy monster with his dramatic black cape and Hungarian accent.

Vampires are known for their speedy healing abilities and can fend off most human diseases. Count Dracula in Stoker's novel also traps his victims with mind control (also called glamouring in modern vampire novels) and the ability to shape-shift, such as into a bat—also a popular characteristic in vampire lore.

But vampires have weaknesses, too. Stoker gave future vampire writers plenty to choose from. He introduced the heart as a vulnerable spot—probably the most popular way of killing a vampire is to stab it through the heart with a wooden stake. Potential victims could also fight off vampires with garlic plants such as wild rose and mountain ash. Stoker's Dracula becomes calm when he touches the beads of a crucifix. The crucifix, as well as other religious items, could also take his power away. Beheading will also stop a vampire in its tracks. Another popular vampire trait is that they are killed by sunlight, but Stoker's count appears during the day on many occasions in *Dracula*. This particular trait was cemented into vampire history by films such as *Nosferatu* (1922).

LAMATSU

Most vampire legends begin in ancient Mesopotamia, four thousand years ago. The Assyrians and Babylonians cowered in fear of a nasty demon goddess named Lamatsu. Her name means "she who erases." She preyed on humans, and legends say that under the cover of darkness Lamatsu would sneak into homes to steal and kill babies, even the unborn! Researchers believe that these stories were created to explain miscarriages and infant deaths. Adults were in danger from this mythical monster, too. Stories of Lamatsu creeping in to suck the blood of young men were told in hushed whispers. The men could be left sterile, with diseases, or plagued by nightmares.

LILITH

Lilith, who is often known as the first woman on Earth, according to Jewish religious texts, is also sometimes credited with being a vampire. She wanted equal standing with Adam because they were created the same way. Some stories tell of Lilith leaving Eden and having many children. God's angels vowed to kill one hundred of her children every day until she returned. Furious, Lilith killed Adam's human children to get back at the angels. Other Lilith stories seem to take their details from the Lamatsu literature. Like

This 1864 birth amulet was created to protect newborns. It depicts an angel and has a spell against the evil eye as well as an incantation against Lilith.

Lamatsu, she has wings and sharp claws. Lilith also steals children, born and unborn, in the dead of night. Lilith appears in the television series *True Blood*, as the very first vampire.

GLOBAL VAMPIRES

Vampire legends appear all over the world. Similar stories show up in the Caribbean in the form of the soucouyant, also known as Ole Higue or Fire Rass depending on the island. By day she is a quiet old woman who often lives alone. But come nightfall she rises as a brilliant, blood-drinking ball of fire that flies through the night in search of her victims.

In China, a kue'i appeared when someone's "lower spirit," or p'o, did not pass into the afterlife, usually because they behaved badly during his or her life. The furious p'o would bring its body back to life and attack people at night. A very nasty version of the kue'i, called a Kuang-shi or Chiang-shi, was covered in white fur and had red eyes that glowed in the night.

STOKER'S INSPIRATIONS

Bram Stoker's *Dracula* came from a nightmare Stoker had about a vampire rising from its tomb. He may have also been inspired by Joseph Sheridan LeFanu's Gothic novel *Carmilla* (1872). In this novel, a woman named Laura befriends and becomes the object of romantic gestures by the female vampire Carmilla. There are also two historical figures who may have provided Stoker with ideas for his book.

Stoker had already outlined the novel when his research unearthed Vlad III Dracula (1431–1476) of Transylvania, a fifteenth-century prince. Also known as Vlad Tepes, he was

THE SCIENCE OF DRACULA

Myths about vampires were likely created to explain various mysteries. The word *vampire* first appears in Europe in the seventeeth and eighteenth centuries. The decomposition of dead bodies may have baffled early civilizations, which created vampire stories to explain the process. When the body shriveled up after death, making teeth and nails more prominent, it may have looked like growing fangs or lengthening claws. A bloated body from gasses released after death might swell organs and make blood seep out of a corpse's lips and mouth.

There were also many stories of "walking corpses" in medieval Europe during times of widespread disease, such as tuberculosis. People blamed the first person to come down with this disease. They decided he or she was a vampire and would drive a stake through his or her heart. Because lots of gases had built up in the dead body, when it was staked it would move and make a groaning sound, terrifying the living!

The disease porphyria has been attributed to some early vampire lore. In one type of this disease (there are three), patients' skin is very fragile and sensitive to light. This has led some to link the disease with early ideas of vampirism. However, the disease has many other un-vampire-like symptoms, which make this link unlikely.

known to be so cruel that he tortured and impaled his victims, even roasting children and feeding them to their mothers before impaling the women. Tepes was rumored to dine among the bodies of his victims, dipping his bread in their blood. In Stoker's novel, it's implied that Tepes was a relative of the count,

This engraving shows Vlad III Dracula enjoying dinner among his victims' impaled bodies as more people are killed. Bram Stoker was inspired by some of these terrifying tales.

but he is called Voivode, not Vlad. For all his violence, Vlad Tepes wanted to be remembered as a saint!

Stoker may have also based his story in part on a Hungarian countess named Elizabeth Báthory. During the sixteenth and seventeenth centuries, she was said to have murdered young women and bathed in their blood in hopes of staying young forever.

STOKER'S STORY

Bram Stoker's novel is widely considered the basis for most modern ideas of vampires in movies and pop culture. Stoker's

FANG FICTION: FIRST VAMPIRE PROSE AND POETRY

Characters with vampire characteristics first appear In eighteenth and nineteenth-century poetry, such as in Heinrich August Ossenfelder's *Der Vampir* (1748) and Lord Byron's *The Giaour* (1813). The first known vampire story ever published was *The Vampyre* (1819) by John Polidori. (This story was written as a competition between Polidori, poet Percy Shelley, and Mary Shelley, who penned the famous novel *Frankenstein* during this competition.) In 1928, Ali Riga Seifi published *Kasigli Voyvode* ("The Impaling Vampire"), the only novel before 1960 that seems to have featured Count Dracula specifically. He makes appearances in short stories, however, including a two-part serial by Ralph Milne Farley called "Another Dracula" for *Weird Tales* (1930).

count is a vampire who travels from his home in Transylvania to England, where he drinks the blood of innocent people to live. The novel is told through diaries and letters written by the main characters: Jonathan Harker, who is the first character to meet the count; Harker's wife, Mina; Dr. Seward; and Lucy Westenra, who eventually becomes a vampire, too. Harker teams up with a Dr. Van Helsing to bring Dracula to his end.

Stoker perpetuated the idea of a vampire that is never seen eating or drinking, never has a shadow, isn't reflected

Jonathan Harker (played by Keanu Reeves) faces off against Dracula (Gary Oldman) in the 1992 movie Dracula, *which is closely based on Stoker's story.*

in mirrors, and must be invited into a building before he can enter. From Stoker, we also get a vampire with tremendous strength, an icy grip, long teeth (fangs), and pointed finger-nails. However, some features from this novel have been dropped from descriptions of the modern monster, such as a long white moustache, bad breath, and hairy palms.

Stoker penned more vampire prose, including a short story collection, *Dracula's Guest, and Other Weird Stories* (1914), as well as other non-vampire fiction.

CHAPTER 2

CHILDREN OF THE NIGHT: EARLY VAMPIRE FILMS

B ram Stoker arranged a dramatic reading of his novel, called *Dracula, or The Undead*, in order to keep anyone from stealing his work. By staging his story, he cemented his rights to its performances. Other Dracula-like stories would have to get his permission or that of his widow to dramatize the popular count.

NOSFERATU (NOSFERATU, EINE SYMPHONIE DES GRAUENS), 1922

In 1922, the earliest known film version based on Stoker's story was produced. A German film company called Prana-Film and a director named Albin Grau loved *Dracula*. Knowing it could be an amazing film, Grau hired a codirector, Friedrich Wilhelm Murnau, and a screenwriter named Henrik Galeen.

Murnau and Galeen created a motion picture quite obviously based on *Dracula*. They changed the title to *Nosferatu*.

In his silent black-and-white film Nosferatu (Nosferatu, eine Symphonie des Grauens), *director Friedrich Wilhelm Murnau used dramatic shadows to chill and thrill rapt audiences.*

Though no one is certain where this word came from, by the time the film was being made, *nosferatu* had come to be associated with the Greek word *nosophoros*, which means plague-carrier. They also changed the setting to Bremen, Germany, in 1838, the date of an actual outbreak of the plague. Names were changed, too, such as Graf Orlock instead of Count Dracula.

It is not clear whether Prana-Film didn't know that they needed to get permission from Stoker's widow, Florence, to make a movie so similar to *Dracula*, or if they didn't

MAX SCHRECK: A REAL-LIFE VAMPIRE?

Actor Max Schreck (1879–1936) played the nightmarish Count Orlock in *Nosferatu*, but the creepiness was not just in the film. To this day, a mist of mysterious rumors swirl around the life of the tall actor whose name in German means "maximum terror." Some stories portrayed Schreck as a real vampire who made a deal with his director Murnau: Schreck would play the part if he could feast on the cast after the movie was made. He played such a convincing Orlock that people thought he must be a vampire! Of course, none of this was true, but *Shadow of a Vampire* (2000), a film supposedly about the making of *Nosferatu*, played up the myth.

In real life, Schreck was known for his talent and his enthusiasm for realistic makeup and creating costumes. He was often offered the parts of strange or very odd characters. Although he went on to work in almost thirty films in his life, he really didn't make a huge splash in the film world after *Nosferatu*. But he acted in many plays in German theater, some with his wife, Fanny Normann. Schreck tended to keep to himself and was known for his strange sense of humor.

Schreck's Count Orlock inspired Stephen King's vampire in *Salem's Lot* and an evil vampire in the video series *Subspecies*. In 1992's *Batman Returns*, Christopher Walken plays a villain named none other than Max Schreck.

Max Schreck's life ended at age fifty-six. He died of a heart attack in Germany in 1936.

Max Schreck played what some say is the creepiest film vampire. In this movie still, Count Orlock is being destroyed by sunlight.

understand the law. But when Florence Stoker found out, she took legal action, claiming copyright infringement. She won her case, and in 1925 *Nosferatu* was ordered to be destroyed. It had already been sent worldwide, so a few copies were saved.

Max Schreck plays an Orlock who looks dramatically different than almost any Dracula. He is bald with long fingernails like claws. Count Orlock's teeth practically jut out of his mouth and he has pointed ears, like a rat. Orlock wears a long coat and has a jerky, awkward walk, not unlike that of a zombie. His odd walk has inspired other monsters on the silver screen, from Franken-stein to the infamous killer Michael in *Halloween* (1978).

F. W. Murnau is sometimes called the greatest German film director of all time, and critics praise his work on this movie. Critics also loved his chilling use of shadow. Most critics now view this film as a masterpiece, but at the time the reviews were split. Felicia Feaster, writing for Turner Classic Movies, notes that when *Nosferatu* was released, "*Variety* praised the film's 'extremely effective symbolism' while *The New York Times* dismissed *Nosferatu* out of hand as a 'would-be spine-chiller.'" Regardless of the reviews, audiences were thrilled by this thriller! And they still are.

DRACULA (1931)

In 1930, Universal Studios officially bought the film rights to *Dracula* from Florence Stoker. They hired Tod Browning to direct it, and it was a perfect film for a director who loved stories about outsiders. Then there was the matter of who would play the great count. The actor Bela Lugosi, who had escaped from Hungary and hardly spoke a word of English had helped Universal convince Stoker's widow to sell them the rights at a lower price. He was expected to get the part, but he was not the first choice for Universal Pictures. In fact, even though Lugosi had played the part many times before in plays produced by Horace Liveright all over the United States, he had to fight for the role! Helen Chandler was cast as Mina with less drama.

Stoker's Count Dracula was described as wearing black from head to toe, but it was Bela Lugosi's formal wear in the 1931 film that cemented what we now consider the classic vampire fashion: a tuxedo paired with a dramatic, flowing opera cape.

Although Lugosi loved playing the part, he later commented that it was both a blessing and a curse. For the rest of his life, Lugosi played very similar characters. Lugosi's son and mother had Lugosi buried in one of his capes. Although he never expressed that desire, they felt he would have appreciated it. His son owns the single remaining official Lugosi cape.

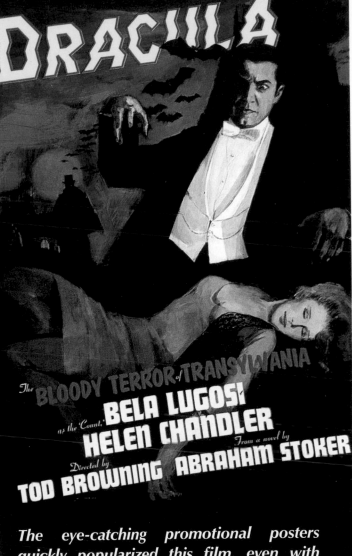

The eye-catching promotional posters quickly popularized this film, even with children. It showed Lugosi as a monstrous, clawing predator and female characters as unsuspecting victims.

Dracula was so popular that it resulted in several sequels: *Dracula's Daughter* (1936), starring Gloria Holden, and *Son of Dracula* (1943), starring Lon Chaney Jr. John Carradine played the count in both *House of Frankenstein* (1944, also starring Boris Karloff and Lon Chaney Jr.) and *House of Dracula* (1945, with Onslow Stevens).

UNDER THE SPELL OF *DRÁCULA*: THE SPANISH FILM

At the same time the American *Dracula* was being filmed, a Spanish-language version, *Drácula*, was being made. In an interview, Lupita Tovar Kohner, who played the character of Eva (Mina in the American film), explains that the American cast and crew worked all day, then the Spanish cast would come in and work all night. At night on the dark set they were "under the spell of Dracula," she explains in the "Introduction to the Spanish Version of *Dracula*" of the *Dracula* Legacy Series DVD. The two crews and casts used the same sets and even the same marks on the floors to indicate where the actors should stand. However, the wardrobes were different for the two films. Kohner noted that the American Mina wore very modest outfits, whereas her own costumes for Eva were far more revealing.

The Spanish version may have had an advantage over the American film. They were able to watch what the Americans filmed each day. This gave them the opportunity to improve on it. Many critics like the lively performance that Carlos

HAMMER HORROR

In 1958, Hammer Films created a gruesome and realistic portrayal of the count in *The Horror of Dracula*, starring Christopher Lee. This film was very graphic and not shy about the sexuality of vampires. *The Horror of Dracula* was such a hit that Hammer went on to offer *The Brides of Dracula* (1960), *Dracula, Prince of Darkness* (1966, again starring Lee), and *Dracula Has Risen From the Grave* (1968), among others, each generally saucier than the last.

Villarías gave as the count (Conde Drácula) under the direction of directors George Melford and Enrique Tovar Ávalos. Some of the visual effects and smooth camera work make critics and film fans prefer the look of the Spanish version. The camera has a more fluid movement, making the dark moods of the story more dynamic. *Drácula* turned out to be one of the last Spanish-language films made in Hollywood.

NEW *NOSFERATU*

In 1979, Count Orlock returned in *Nosferatu: The Vampyre* (Originally titled *Nosferatu: Phantom der Nacht*). This *Nosferatu* remake was written, produced, and directed by Werner Herzog and featured Klaus Kinski as the creepy Count Orlock. It kept the same basic storyline as the 1922 film, but it restored the names to those used in Stoker's novel, this time with permission. In 1988 an Italian sequel was made, called *Vampire in Venice*.

Christopher Lee starred as the count in **The Horror of Dracula** *(1958) for Hammer Films. Hammer produced graphic seductive vampire films that delighted the audiences.*

 E. Elias Merhige created the film *Shadow of the Vampire* (2000) out of respect to Murnau and *Nosferatu*. This film is a comedy that takes a look at the making of the movie. Willem Dafoe played Max Schreck and won an Oscar for Best Supporting Actor for his performance.

CHAPTER 3

MORE CHILDREN OF THE NIGHT: MODERN VAMPIRES

On September 27, 1949, Bela Lugosi performed as a guest star on *The Texaco Star Theater*, becoming the first person to appear on television dressed as a vampire, although he was not specifically called Dracula on the program. Vampires didn't become part of regular television entertainment until the early 1950s, however, because television was supposed to amuse, not frighten, viewers.

VAMPIRES FOR THE VERY YOUNG

Most vampire movies and stories are created for an adult audience, but as the first popular fang film, *Dracula*, showed, kids have always loved the story! It wasn't until 1971 that the first novel with a vampire theme was written just for a young audience. *Danger on Vampire Trail* (Hardy Boys, #50, 1971) was part of the mystery series by Franklin W. Dixon. Angela

They're Not Just Best Friends.
They're Blood Brothers.

The Little Vampire

In 2000 **The Little Vampire** *film finally brought the popular kids' book series, originally published in 1979, to the silver screen. It was also a television series in 1986.*

Sommer-Bodenburg's twenty-book series *The Little Vampire*, the first of which was published in 1979, inspired a movie of the same name that was released in 2000.

On the cuddlier side, children's authors Deborah and Frank Howe created *Bunnicula* (1979) about a fanged vampire bunny that sleeps all day and sucks the juice out of vegetables. Frank continued the book as a series, which ended with *Bunnicula Meets Edgar Allen Crow* in 2006. He also did picture book spin-offs for even younger readers, *Tales from the House of Bunnicula* and *Bunnicula*

COUNTING WITH COUNT VON COUNT

Sesame Street's Count von Count lives in a castle, has bats for pets, wears a cape that Bela Lugosi would love, and has fangs.

It's true, the purple puppet does not have many of the vampire's nastier habits, like drinking blood, but he has an obvious attraction to counting. *Sesame Street* didn't invent this fascination with numbers just to teach kids to count. A common vampire weakness in legends is a compulsive need to count things, also known as arithmomania. In pre-modern days when most people feared that vampires were a real threat, they would sprinkle rice or poppy seeds all over the floor. When the vampire entered their homes, they thought it would be unable to resist counting every last seed or grain. This distraction would leave enough time for the humans to escape or the sun to rise.

and Friends. A television cartoon, *Bunnicula, the Vampire Rabbit*, aired in 1982.

Other cartoon vampires include a small purple vampire named Little Gruesome in Hanna-Barbera Productions' *Wacky Races* (1968–1970), *Archie's Weird Mysteries: Archie and the Riverdale Vampires* (2001), and *Scooby-Doo and the Legend of the Vampire* (2003), just to name a few.

Sesame Street's cast of muppets includes Count von Count (although he's never actually called a vampire), who counts everything he can, whether it's his pet bats or bananas. And kids' breakfast cereals even get in on the vampire trend with Count Chocula.

VAMPIRES IN THE LIVING ROOM

In the 1960s, television started to include vampires as characters in leading roles. *The Addams Family* (1964–1966) on ABC was based on the Charles Addams cartoon featured in the *New Yorker* magazine. The curvy and feisty Morticia Addams was played by Carolyn Jones and later by Ellie Harvey in *The New Addams Family* (1998–1999). Morticia was not specifically called a vampire, but her gothic appearance, with pale skin and long, black dresses, made the suggestion.

Another successful series was *The Munsters* (1964–1966) on CBS, which centered on a wacky family that included a vampire duo. Yvonne de Carlo played Lily Munster and Al Lewis was Grandpa Munster. As the series progressed, viewers found out that Grandpa was supposed to be Count Dracula!

DARK SHADOWS

In 1966, television viewers were introduced to the Collins family in *Dark Shadows* (starring Jonathan Frid and Grayson Hall). At first, it was just a gothic daytime drama, but when ratings were poor, they added some ghosts. However, it was the addition of the vampire that really made the show a success. Teens rushed home from school to see the next episode. Jonathan Frid played the unhappy vampire named Barnabas Collins. The show boasts 1,200 episodes, and it ran until 1972. In 1991 a *Dark Shadows* miniseries aired, featuring Ben Cross and Joanna Going. *Dark Shadows* also made it to the silver screen, with *House of Dark Shadows* in 1970, starring Jonathan Frid and Grayson Hall, and a remake of the original television series in 2012, starring Johnny Depp and Michelle Pfeiffer. Cross, Depp, and Frid all sport a long black Lugosi-style cape in their Barnabas Collins characterizations. Depp in particular wears a long black cape and even a medallion, as did Lugosi in 1931, and has long nails not unlike Orlock in *Nosferatu*.

BUFFY THE VAMPIRE SLAYER

In 1992 director Fran Rubel Kuzui and writer Joss Whedon brought a new vampire story to the silver screen: *Buffy the Vampire Slayer*, starring Kristy Swanson and Donald Sutherland. Buffy is a teenage girl who learns she is the chosen one of all vampire slayers. The film's reviews were mixed, but moviegoers loved it. Five years later, *Buffy* came to television, this time with Whedon as director and starring Sara Michelle Geller as Buffy Summers and David Boreanaz as her love interest Angel, who is inconveniently a vampire with a soul. Buffy slayed vampires and all kinds

Sara Michelle Geller played the butt-kicking vampire slayer Buffy Summers in the **Buffy the Vampire Slayer** *television series.*

of monsters for seven seasons. In an episode in 2000 titled "Buffy v. Dracula," Buffy faces off with none other than Count Dracula himself! The show also featured a super-vampire called the Master, with pale skin that hinted back to *Nosferatu*.

A darker spin-off, *Angel*, again starring Boreanaz, hit the airwaves in 1999. Other characters from the Buffy show appeared, and occasional appearances were made by Geller.

In 2007, Dark Horse Comics published the series *Buffy the Vampire Slayer* Season Eight, which continued where the television show left off. Angel was also popular enough to result in several books and comics, including the comic book series *Angel, After the Fall* by Brian Lynch in 2008, which also picks up where the television show left off.

True Blood's *stars were the tough and telepathic southern belle Sookie Stackhouse (Anna Paquin) and vampire Bill Compton (Stephen Moyer). The HBO drama emphasized the violence and sex of vampire lore.*

TRUE BLOOD

HBO's *True Blood* came about in part thanks to the comparatively tame *Buffy*. With its darker, sexier, and more violent themes, it appealed to an older audience but was likely just as popular as *Buffy*. Based loosely on *The Southern Vampire Mysteries* series of novels by Charlaine Harris, this series ran from 2008 to 2014. The main character, Sookie Stackhouse (played by Anna Paquin), is a telepathic waitress in Bon Temps, Louisiana. When she meets Bill Compton (played by Stephen Moyer), a 173-year-old vampire, she discovers the one man who can resist her telepathic talents.

Although the vampires in this series stay pretty traditional—they can't go out in the light and can glamour humans (a vampire trick to hypnotize victims)—Harris added a synthetic blood called "tru blood," which allows vampires to live with humans without fear of needing to drink their blood. In the fifth and sixth seasons, the series adds Lilith, who is said to be the original vampire. She tells Bill, "God made me as vampire, and Adam and Eve as human. I am worshiped as a god as some may come to worship you as a god. But there is no god but God." (Lilith has also made appearances in other vampire literature, such as the Marvel Comic *Morbius the Living Vampire*).

THE VAMPIRE DIARIES

A series called *The Vampire Diaries* (2009–), based on the book series by L. J. Smith, is geared toward a younger audience without as much violence and sexual content. Its series premier was viewed by 4.8 million in the United States. *The Vampire Diaries* has won numerous awards, as well as a nomination for the 2015 People's Choice Award for Favorite Network Sci-Fi/ Fantasy TV Show.

FANG FILM

By now, the library of vampire- and Dracula-related movies is almost more than anyone could manage to watch, even if you had every night for the rest of time to do it! So let's just take a look at a few.

THE LOST BOYS

The 1980s brought the vampire film into a slightly edgier, practically punk genre with *The Lost Boys* (1987), with its tag line "Being wild is in their blood." In this horror comedy, a single mother, Lucy (perhaps a nod to the character in Stoker's

THE LOST BOYS

Kiefer Sutherland played a vampire bad boy in the 1987 The Lost Boys. *The vampires in this fun and funky flick were a change from formal Dracula dramas.*

story), moves to a new town in California with her two sons, played by Jason Patric and Corey Haim. Soon the boys realize that there is more to the motorcycle gangs in their new neighborhood than meets the eye.

Like Stoker's vampires, *The Lost Boys* vampires come out only at night (in fact, the actors are rumored to have done the same while they were filming, even covering their windows so they could sleep during the day). It sneered at the glamour and capes of Bela Lugosi and took on punk hair and clothes. In his article for the Total Film website, Josh Winning calls it "a vampire flick made back when vampire flicks weren't known for being edgy and fun." In this film, the vampires look like normal human beings…until they're on the hunt, when their faces become monstrous with white or blood-red eyes and sharp, grotesque features. It is an idea that Joss Whedon later used in his *Buffy* series with the character Angel.

The Lost Boys was also written as a novella in 1987 by author Craig Shaw Gardner. It includes scenes that were dropped from the film as well as some new vampire lore, such as vampires being unable to cross running water. *The Lost Boys* film won the Saturn Award for Best Horror Film in 1988.

INTERVIEW WITH THE VAMPIRE

Anne Rice's popular *Vampire Chronicles* novels began with *Interview with the Vampire* in 1976, which is credited with reviving vampire stories for a modern audience. Without her work, many believe there would be no *Buffy, True Blood,* or *Twilight.* This first novel was made into a film of the same name in 1994, starring Brad Pitt and Tom Cruise. The third book in the series, *Queen of the Damned,* published in 1988, was made into a movie of the same name in 2002, starring pop star Aaliyah in the title role. The film was released six months after Aaliyah's untimely death. In 2014, Rice released the eleventh book in the series, *Prince Lestat.* That same year, Universal Studios bought the rights to all of the books in the *Vampire Chronicles* series with the intention of making more movies.

TWILIGHT

One of the more recent films to get people talking about vampires is *The Twilight Saga* series (2008–2012), five films based on Stephenie Meyer's four-book series: *Twilight, New Moon, Eclipse,* and *Breaking Dawn.* (*Breaking Dawn* was released in two parts.) The *Twilight* books and movie focus on a budding love between a high school student Isabella (Bella) Swan (played by Kristin Stewart) and the 108-year-old vampire Edward Cullen (played by Robert Pattinson). *Twilight* vampires are described as having extreme beauty, and once a human is turned into a vampire he or she becomes even more attractive—practically perfect.

The vampires in this series do stay true to a few Stoker qualities, such as showing fangs when they turn into vampires and surviving only on blood. However, Meyer's vampires are able to go out in the daylight. But because they sparkle in the sun, staying out of direct light allows them to keep their secret safe. The vampires in the Cullen family also feed on animals rather than humans and are immune to crucifixes and holy water.

DRACULA UNTOLD

Dracula Untold (2014) goes back to the turn of the century and Vlad the Impaler's history. The movie's website describes it as "the origin story of the man who became Dracula," and the critics generally agreed. *Dracula Untold* was an action film rather than horror. This PG-13 movie only suggested some of the violence that made the historical Vlad (played by Luke Evans) quite famous in history. And although some parts of the story agree with history, *Time* magazine's entertainment writer Richard Corliss comments that it depicts "Vlad as a loving husband, a protective father and a national hero."

CHAPTER 4

TRULY UNDEAD MONSTERS

Vampire stories have remained very popular through several generations. With more than two hundred interpretations of the count in film alone, Dracula is the most popular horror film character of all time. Modern styles have also taken up vampire stories, with undead creatures gracing the pages of comic books, appearing in musicals, and even being choreographed into a ballet. The vampire genre, it seems, won't die anytime soon. The only question is, where will vampires show up next?

BEAUTY AND THE BEAST

Today's Dracula characters are far more physically appealing than Max Schreck's *Nosferatu* and even Bram Stoker's hairy-palmed creature with halitosis. Stoker's Dracula becomes younger as he drinks blood, but not better looking. More recent vampires tend to be handsome, sympathetic characters, such as Bill Compton and Eric Northman in *True Blood* and Edward Cullen and the vampires of *Twilight*.

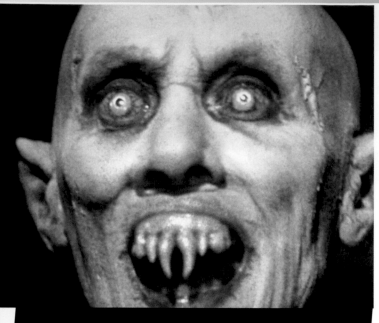

In King's novel and the 1979 film Salem's Lot, vampires looked like authentic, scary monsters.

Not all of today's modern bloodsuckers are pretty boys, however. Horror author extraordinaire Stephen King's book *Salem's Lot* harkens back to the more "authentic" book-based Dracula. He remembers:

One of the novels I taught was Dracula. I was surprised at how vital it had remained over the years; the kids liked it, and I liked it, too. One night over supper I wondered aloud what would happen if Dracula came back in the twentieth century, to America. "He'd probably be run over by a Yellow Cab on Park Avenue and killed," my wife said.... But if he were to show up in a sleepy little country town, what then? I decided I wanted to find out, so I wrote 'Salem's Lot, which was originally titled Second Coming.

The vampires of Guillermo del Toro's trilogy *The Strain* (2009–2011), as well as the television series based on the

NEW ORLEANS: VAMPIRE CITY

New Orleans has a rich history with vampire stories. It has hosted its own Vampire Film Festival, which included films, discussions with authors, and even a ball! New Orleans is the "true American vampire city," according to J. Gordon Melton, author of *The Vampire Book: The Encyclopedia of the Undead*, and with good reason. Both Anne Rice and Charlaine Harris set their stories in this city. The movies based on Rice's novels and Harris's television series *True Blood* were filmed in and around New Orleans.

books, are some gross ghouls. Molly Osberg, editor and writer for the Verge website, writes that "vampires don't look like pop stars and sip blood from champagne flutes; they rip your throat out…" And not much is pretty about that!

CREATURES IN THE COMICS

The comic book world has loved Dracula and vampire stories, too. The first vampire to bare his pointy teeth in comics was the Vampire Master. He appeared in a four-part DC Comics series from 1935 to 1936, starting with *More Fun Comics No. 6: The Vampire Master Part 1*. The first time Dracula himself appeared in a comic was in 1951 in *Eerie No. 8*.

But vampires were banned from comic books in 1954 by the Comic Magazine Association of America, and they weren't allowed out of the coffin again until 1972. The ban was all thanks to

Wesley Snipes starred in Marvel Comics' Blade trilogy. African American Blade was uniquely half-vampire and half-human, so he was not limited to going out only at night.

the idea that they were too violent and sexy and thus a bad influence on young minds. A similar ban was applied in the United Kingdom.

Marvel Comics created *Morbius, the Living Vampire* in 1971 and released it after the ban was lifted. *Fray: Future Slayer* (by Joss Whedon, of *Buffy the Vampire Slayer* fame) and *Buffy the Vampire Slayer* both tackled vampires among the comic strips, too. There's even a vampire cow out there in comic land in *Hellcow*.

And speaking of vampire slayers, there's Blade. He's an African American, as well as half vampire and half human. So he can walk about during the day. Blade first appears in the Marvel Comic *The Tomb of Dracula #10* (1973). He goes on to star in his own series of comic books and then a trilogy of movies: *Blade* (1998), *Blade II* (2002), and *Blade: Trinity* (2004) with Wesley Snipes in the title role. This was followed by a short-lived series, *Blade: The Series* (2006), starring Sticky Fingaz. *The Vampire Book* author J. Gordon Melton describes Blade as "evil, but with some traits of human feeling, pining over love betrayed...."

DRACULA STAGED

Dracula's fierce fangs have even been interpreted into dance all over the world. Canada's Royal Winnipeg Ballet performed a full-length ballet created by choreographer Mark Godden. Later, it was adapted for film as *Dracula: Pages from a Virgin's Diary*. *Dracula, the Musical*, based on the Stoker's novel, is also widely performed.

Count Dracula, whether he's depicted in the movies or elsewhere, continues to fascinate and frighten. But before you decide whether or not you truly believe in vampires, consider these parting words from Van Helsing, spoken at the end of the 1931 film: "Just a moment, ladies and gentlemen! Just a word before you go. We hope the memories of Dracula and Renfield won't give you bad dreams, so just a word of reassurance. When you get home tonight and the lights have been turned down and you are afraid to look behind the curtains and you dread to see a face appear at the window—why, just pull yourself together and remember that after all there are such things."

FILMOGRAPHY

Nosferatu (Nosferatu, eine Symphonie des Grauens) (1922)
Directed by F. W. Murnau. Starring Max Schreck and Greta Schröder.

Dracula (1931)
Directed by Tod Browning. Starring Bela Lugosi and Helen Chandler.

Dracula's Daughter (1936)
Directed by Lambert Hillyer. Starring Otto Kruger and Gloria Holden.

Son of Dracula (1943)
Directed by Robert Siodmak. Starring Lon Chaney Jr. and Robert Paige.

House of Frankenstein (1944)
Directed by Erle C. Kenton. Starring Boris Karloff and Lon Chaney Jr.

House of Dracula (1945)
Directed by Erle C. Kenton. Starring Onslow Stevens and John Carradine.

The Horror of Dracula (1958)
Directed by Terence Fisher. Starring Peter Cushing and Christopher Lee.

House of Dark Shadows (1970)
Directed by Dan Curtis. Starring Jonathan Frid and Grayson Hall.

Blacula (1972)
Directed by William Crain. Starring William Marshall and Vonetta McGee.

Dracula A.D. 1972 (1972)
Directed by Alan Gibson. Starring Christopher Lee and Peter Cushing.

Nosferatu the Vampyre (1979)
Directed by Werner Herzog. Starring Klaus Kinski and Isabelle Adjani.

The Lost Boys (1987)
Directed by Joel Schumacher. Starring Jason Patric and Corey Haim.

Bram Stoker's Dracula (1992)
Directed by Francis Ford Coppola. Starring Gary Oldman and Winona Ryder.

Buffy the Vampire Slayer (1992)
Directed by Fran Rubel Kuzui. Starring Kristy Swanson and Donald Sutherland.

Interview with the Vampire: The Vampire Chronicles (1994)
Directed by Neil Jordan. Starring Brad Pitt and Tom Cruise.

Blade (1998)
Directed by Stephen Norrington. Starring Wesley Snipes and Stephen Dorff.

The Little Vampire (2000)
Directed by Uli Edel. Starring Jonathan Lipnicki and Rollo Weeks.

Shadow of the Vampire (2000)
Directed by E. Elias Merhige. Starring John Malkovich and Willem Dafoe.

Dracula: Pages from a Virgin's Diary (2002)
Directed by Guy Maddin. Starring Wei-Qiang Zhang and Tara Birtwhistle.

Blade II (2002)
Directed by Guillermo del Toro. Starring Wesley Snipes and Kris Kristofferson.

Blade: Trinity (2004)
Directed by David S. Goyer. Starring Wesley Snipes and Kris Kristofferson.

Twilight (2008)
Directed by Catherine Hardwicke. Starring Kristen Stewart and Robert Pattinson.

New Moon (2009)
Directed by Chris Weitz. Starring Kristen Stewart and Robert Pattinson.

Eclipse (2010)
Directed by David Slade. Starring Kristen Stewart and Robert Pattinson.

Breaking Dawn Part 1 (2011)
Directed by Bill Condon. Starring Kristen Stewart and Robert Pattinson.

Breaking Dawn Part 2 (2012)
Directed by Bill Condon. Starring Kristen Stewart and Robert Pattinson.

Dark Shadows (2012)
Directed by Tim Burton. Starring Johnny Depp and Michelle Pfeiffer.

Dracula: The Dark Prince (2013)
Directed by Pearry Reginald Teo. Starring Luke Roberts and Jon Voight.

Dracula Untold (2014)
Directed by Gary Shore. Starring Luke Evans and Dominic Cooper.

GLOSSARY

ARITHMOMANIA An obsession with counting.

CHOREOGRAPHER One who creates and arranges dances and dance steps.

CRUCIFIX A symbol of the cross with a figure of Jesus on it.

DECOMPOSITION Rotting or breaking down.

GOTHIC Dark and gloomy; belonging to the dark ages.

GRUESOME Causing horror or disgust.

LORE Information or traditions about a subject.

MISCARRIAGE A medical condition in which a pregnancy ends too early for the baby to survive.

MOUNTAIN ASH A small tree in the rose family.

PORPHYRIA A rare blood disease in which a person's ability to produce red blood cells is limited.

PREINDUSTRIAL Having to do with a time before industry was built up.

PREMATURE Occurring too soon.

SPIN-OFF Something inspired by or marketed because of its relationship to a popular movie, book, or television show.

STERILITY The characteristic of being unable to reproduce.

SYMPATHETIC Friendly or enjoyable.

SYNTHETIC Made from chemicals.

TELEPATHIC Able to read minds.

TRILOGY A collection of three, usually novels, films, or plays.

TUBERCULOSIS A spreadable disease of the lungs.

FOR MORE INFORMATION

American Film Institute

2021 N Western Avenue

Los Angeles, CA 90027

(323) 856-7600

Website: http://www.afi.com

The American Film Institute seeks to protect the history of films like *Dracula*, to honor artists and their work, and to educate future filmmakers.

The Dracula Library

Center for Studies on New Religions

Via Confienza 19

10121 Torino

Italy

Website: http://www.cesnur.org/dracula_library.htm

The Dracula Library is the largest public library of vampire books, including books about vampires as well as books by authors of vampire-related books.

North American Victorian Studies Association

Dept. of English

Purdue University

500 Oval Drive

West Lafayette, IN 47907

Website: http://navsa.org

The North American Victorian Studies Association was founded to offer a forum for discussion about Victorian literature, such as *Dracula*.

The Transylvania Society of Dracula: Canadian Chapter

P.O. Box 23240

Churchill Square P.O.

St. John's, NF A1B 4J9

Canada

This international nonprofit organization studies Vlad (Tepes) Dracula as well as Count Dracula. The original chapter was formed in Romania.

WEBSITES

Because of the changing nature of Internet links, Rosen Publishing has developed an online list of websites related to the subject of this book. This site is updated regularly. Please use this link to access the list:

http://www.rosenlinks.com/GMM/Drac

FOR FURTHER READING

Abele, Robert. *The Twilight Saga: The Complete Film Archive: Memories, Mementos, and Other Treasures from the Creative Team Behind the Beloved Motion Pictures.* New York, NY: Little, Brown, 2012.

Beresford, Matthew. *From Demons to Dracula: The Creation of the Modern Vampire Myth.* London, England: Reaktion Books, 2009.

Bringle, Jennifer. *Vampires in Film and Television.* New York, NY: Rosen Publishing, 2011.

Burgan, Michael. *Dracula's Dark World* (Horrorscapes). New York, NY: Bearport, 2010.

Hellman, Roxanne, and Derek Hall. *Vampire Legends and Myths* (Supernatural). New York, NY: Rosen Publishing, 2011.

Indovino, Saina C. *Dracula and Beyond: Famous Vampires & Werewolves in Literature and Film* (Making of a Monster: Vampires & Werewolves). Broomall, PA: Mason Crest, 2010.

Kaplan, Arie. *Vampires: Dracula: The Life of Vlad the Impaler.* New York, NY: Rosen Central, 2011.

Klinger, Leslie S. *In the Shadow of Dracula.* San Diego, CA: IDW, 2011.

Roberts, Steven. *Vampires!* New York, NY: Rosen Publishing, 2012.

Sims, Michael, ed. *Dracula's Guest: A Connoisseur's Collection of Victorian Vampire Stories.* New York, NY: Walker and Company, 2010.

Stewart, Gail. *Vampires: Do They Exist?* (The Vampire Library). San Diego, CA: ReferencePoint, 2010.

Stoker, Bram. *The New Annotated Dracula.* Edited by Leslie Klinger. New York, NY: Norton, 2008.

Thomas, Roy. *Dracula* (Marvel Classics). New York, NY: Marvel, 2010.

Weingarten, Ethan. *Transylvania.* New York, NY: Gareth Stevens, 2014.

Woog, Adam. *Vampires in the Movies* (Vampire Library). San Diego, CA: ReferencePoint, 2010.

BIBLIOGRAPHY

Atkinson, Michael. "A Bloody Disgrace." *Guardian*, January 25, 2001. Retrieved November 8, 2014 (http://www.theguardian.com).

Clark, Josh. "Who Was the Real Count Dracula?" Retrieved November 15, 2014 (http://history.howstuffworks.com).

Corliss, Richard. "The Vampire as Messiah in Dracula Untold." *Time*, October 12, 2014. Retrieved November 12, 2014 (http://time.com).

Feaster, Felicia. "Nosferatu." TCM. Retrieved November 6, 2014 (http://www .tcm.com/this-month/article/437|0/Nosferatu.html).

Graham, Dave. "Book Lifts Lid on Star of Eerie First Dracula Film." Reuters, May 9, 2008. Retrieved November 15, 2014 (http://www.reuters.com).

History.com "Was Dracula a Real Person?" May 22, 2013. Retrieved November 15, 2014 (http://www.history.com).

Huber, Jennifer. "Science Behind Vampire Myths." Quest, October 29, 2012. Retrieved November 15, 2014 (http://science.kqed.org).

IMDb. "Nosferatu the Vampyre." Retrieved November 15, 2014 (http://www .imdb.com/title/tt0079641/?ref_=nm_knf_i2).

King, Stephen. "'Salem's Lot." Stephen King Official Website. 2014. Retrieved November 15, 2014 (http://stephenking.com).

Melton, J. Gordon, Ph.D. *The Vampire Book: The Encyclopedia of the Undead*. Third ed. Canton, MI: Visible Ink, 2014.

Osberg, Molly. "Special Vampires Unit: Guillermo del Toro's 'The Strain' is 'CSI' with the Undead." The Verge, July 12, 2014. Retrieved November 15, 2014 (http://www.theverge.com).

Universal Studios. *Dracula: The Universal Legacy Collection*. DVD. 2004.

Winning, Josh. "The Story Behind The Lost Boys." Total Film, March 11, 2010. Retrieved November 11, 2014 (http://www.totalfilm.com).

Zalben, Alex. "The 10 Best Vampires in Comics." MTV Geek News, February 24, 2011. Retrieved November 15, 2014 (http://geek-news.mtv .com/2011/02/24/the-10-best-vampires-in-comics).

INDEX

ABOUT THE AUTHOR

Heather Moore Niver is a writer and editor living in New York State. Among many other titles, such as *20 Fun Facts About Bats*, she has written a deliciously gory book called *Digging Up the Dead: Executions and Sacrifices*.

PHOTO CREDITS